And No Net Ensnares Me

Rana Shubair

Fomite
Burlington, VT

ISBN- 13: 978-1-959984-33-7
Library of Congress Control Number: 2023945362

Fomite
58 Peru Street
Burlington, VT 05401
www.fomitepress.com

02-16-2026

To the freedom fighters who light the path to freedom

"Freedom beckons along the horizon afar,
Leading our footsteps, like the polar star."
— Mahmoud Darwish

Chapter 1

Fatina: Secrets

FATINA WAS SNOOPING through one of Abdullah's notebooks, reading an entry about Omar.

> *"I wanted to thank you for visiting me in my dreams. Last night, I saw you in a lush green field. It was so vast, with no beginning and no end. I saw you from afar. I called your name, but you just stood there. I ran towards you as I kept calling, and then, when I was only a few feet away, you turned around. I saw your face! I can't tell you how much I've missed your beautiful face. But in the dream, your smile was different; your features weren't the same as when you were here."*

Fatina's heart throbbed. Even after all these years, Abdullah still missed his comrade, Omar. She questioned if time was a healer after all.

Abdullah's voice broke her reverie. His eyes were fixed on the notebook, his expression impassive. He held out his hand. "Please," he said sternly.

Flushing, Fatina arranged the pencil holder, stationery, and books, then shut the notebook and pushed it aside, her eyes not meeting his. Her cheeks were on fire.

"I've told you before not to go through my notebooks."

Fatina was sick of the idea of confidential material. Maybe it was because she didn't keep any secret diaries. She had even shared with Abdullah her most naïve teenage thoughts and pranks, her favorite Turkish movie star, and the songs she loved most.

The only thing she kept from him was the number of men who had come to ask for her hand before him—some of whom Abdullah would have known. As the proposals came in, Fatina had told her parents she wasn't interested in marriage. She'd already envisioned her handsome husband, and Abdullah was everything she could've asked for.

"You're a well of secrets again!" she fumed, leaping off the chair and stomping past him.

Fatina hated how easily she unraveled, especially because she had made it her mission to be strong in the face of adversity. She lived in a world where life's trials were anything but ordinary, leaving no room for feeble attitudes. Military attacks. Unpredictable shelling or bombing. Frantic fleeing in the middle of the night or broad daylight. Always searching for safety when there was none. Surviving all that had taught her resilience, but loving a man who kept his inner life sealed away required a strength she was still learning.

In her room, Fatina opened the closet, grabbed two shelves of clothes, and flung them on the floor. She scolded herself for being so connected to Abdullah's world of writing and his comings and goings. She'd just made an idiot of herself.

Sitting amongst the pile of clothes, Fatina knew conquering her insecurities and fears was a constant battle—one that surfaced most when she felt herself falling short. She often measured her strength against the powerful women she had grown up watching, the ones who stood up to soldiers barging into their homes at night, trying to take their sons. Could she ever be like them? Her kids needed her to be strong, yet her self-confidence still wavered.

Even as she muttered expletives about her stupidity, Fatina also recognized one truth: she could never hide her vulnerability from Abdullah. She needed to be herself with someone, and he was that person.

She picked up a T-shirt, folded the right-arm panel over and back, then the left, but it was nowhere near neat. Her injured hand always slowed her down, refusing to obey the way it once had. *Astagfirullah*, she sighed, looking heavenward.

The damage had been done years ago, early in their marriage. Abdullah had been on duty that night, leaving Fatina alone at home. She was trying to focus on her studies when Israeli warplanes roared overhead. An enormous explosion followed, rocking the area and shattering the bedroom windows. Glass flew everywhere. Shards tore into her hand, destroying tissue and leaving it permanently maimed.

Before she could straighten the pile of clothes, Abdullah appeared in the doorway. Leaning against the frame, he paused as if he were calculating his move. Then he unbuttoned his shirt, took it off, placed it on the bed, and sat on the floor beside Fatina. He picked up a pair of black satin shorts. "You used to love wearing these…" he said as he held up the tiny garment to his nose and inhaled deeply.

"I used to be many things," she said, pretending to be engrossed in arranging her clothes.

"Lulu, I'm sorry. There's something on my mind. That's all."

"Of course. Something secretive," she said matter-of-factly, her hands moving quickly and nervously, folding and refolding garments. Although she was upset with Abdullah, she was angrier with herself. Tears started streaming down her face, making her choke on her own words. "It's your life…your writing, your diaries, and all that. I'm the one constantly interfering…" Fatina stopped as she pressed a shirt against her mouth.

"No. Don't say that… you know I ask you to read my stuff and give me your opinion." He brought Fatina's mangled hand to his lips and kissed it, the way he always did—careful, reverent.

Fatina's voice quavered. "I have nothing good to do in my life anymore. I just sit at home and do what I do every day. I'm as useless as a piece of old furniture. And I'm constantly worried about…"

Abdullah sat with his back against the closet and pulled her close. He rested his chin on her head and rubbed her back. Warmth radiated from his body, comforting Fatina. She felt safe. Her breathing relaxed a bit, and he whispered, "What are you worried about?" His voice was calm and soothing.

"You know…" she said, barely audible, beset with shame.

It was always the same with Fatina. If it wasn't her insecurities about Abdullah, it was the constant fear of military operations and the venomous rumors about impending attacks.

Once, she was at her parents' place when her mother had a few guests over. Fatina had gone to make them coffee, and when she came back, they were talking about fears of another war. One of the women gaped, making sure the horror was conveyed and said, "They say the Israelis are getting ready for another war. And it's going to be fiercer than the last one." Fatina had stopped dead in her tracks. Her hands had started shaking, and the tray of coffee cups crashed to the floor.

Chapter 2

Abdullah: Writers' Club

ABDULLAH STOOD in front of the mirror, combing his hair. It was straight, dark brown, and kept short. Fatina always told him she loved how it waved back and forth as she ran her fingers through it when Abdullah lay across her lap.

"This movement soothes me, Abood," she would say. "Do you like it?"

"It's like a lullaby. Makes me sleepy."

He picked up his second favorite cologne. It only had a few sprays left. He sprayed it on his neck, left and right. His favorite was Calvin Klein, but that was reserved for intimate moments with Fatina.

She had made it clear that she wouldn't tolerate any other woman getting a whiff of it as her husband passed by. "You're one jealous baby," he teased her once. "So even if any woman out there does smell it, you think she'll get bewitched and try to hunt me down?"

Abdullah cherished Fatina. He could see she didn't realize how possessive she had become of him. She'd said it before, though: having to share him with their homeland was one thing, but his heart could belong only to her.

"I trust you, Aboodi, you know that," she said, trying to downplay her jealousy. "But I don't trust lots of women out there, especially ones who chase married men."

"I'm not easy to catch, so relax." Abdullah engulfed Fatina in a warm embrace and whispered in her ear, "And where do you get such ideas?"

"From stories I hear," she confessed. Abdullah gently released Fatina. She avoided his gaze and busied herself with his shirt buttons.

"Is there gossip circulating about me?" He pushed a strand of hair behind her ear.

"Not really, but sometimes I wander off in my mind..." Fatina replied. "You know, men who take another wife…"

Her words lingered, but Abdullah gazed at her warmly. Twelve years of marriage bonded them in an unbreakable way. They had their little fights, usually sparked by Abdullah's absences. But he made up for the long hours away by spending Fridays at home and finding quiet moments just for the two of them. He hoped she felt reassured, though he knew hearing it from his lips would make it real.

Love for Fatina flowed through his veins, and he could never think of loving another woman. He felt content with the love they shared, grateful for it in every way. She had been an ordinary girl when he proposed to her. But while she didn't come from a well-known family, her kindness, beauty, and the way she cared for others drew him in completely. That she accepted the idea of marrying a Resistance fighter only increased his love.

It was moments like these, intimate and unguarded, that reminded him why he cherished their bond so profoundly.

"Can you look me in the eye when you say that?" Abdullah challenged her.

She quickly conceded, wrapping her arms around him and resting against his chest while she stroked his arm. "I'm sorry," she said, her voice breaking.

"You know I love you," he whispered, drawing her closer. That was all he needed to say.

Today, Abdullah was getting ready for a new experience. He had signed up for a writers' club, where he'd discuss writing-related topics and possibly find some respite in the change of atmosphere. Although the club was completely unrelated to his work in the Resistance, he needed to pursue his other passions. He always felt that writing was a way to release energy and feel better.

Abdullah hadn't told Fatina about the club yet. She came into the room to find him putting on his long-sleeved white linen shirt, which he had just ironed meticulously.

When they first got married, Abdullah tried to teach Fatina how to iron. Before that, her brothers had nagged her to iron their clothes, but she avoided it by saying they'd do a better job themselves. And the proof was that, in Gaza, it was men who ironed at laundromats.

Abdullah rolled his sleeves up to his elbows.

"Where are you going dressed so provocatively, my love?" Fatina teased. "Showing off your masculinity."

"To a writers' club. Isn't that great for a change?"

He didn't have to wait long for a response. Fatina raised her eyebrows. "Abood, you can't be serious!"

"Why? Am I good only for tunnel work?"

Abdullah knew his wife had never been fascinated by his work in the tunnels and wished he had an ordinary desk job as an accountant or something. For Resistance fighters, the tunnels meant long hours away from home, working under precarious conditions that stirred grief and painful memories of comrades who had died underground. Abdullah had eventually quit and never fully recovered after Ahmed died down there.

"I'm just trying to say I'm impressed by your new interests," she said. "And I can't help being envious. Is it an all-male gathering or will there be sophisticated female writers, so to speak?"

Abdullah grabbed his car keys. "I don't know. I'll tell you all about it when I get back." He gave her a quick peck on her lips. Fatina didn't let go easily. "Wait up for me." Abdullah winked, then hurried out.

Chapter 3

Abdullah: First Meeting

ABDULLAH ARRIVED ten minutes early. He walked into the library where the meeting was to convene, but no one was in sight. Very typical of Gazans, he thought, but certainly not for him. Being in the Resistance had taught him to be extra punctual.

His commanding officer, Dirgham, didn't tolerate even a minute's delay. Abdullah learned this the hard way when he arrived six minutes late on his first day of recruitment. A forty-five-year-old veteran who had spent twenty-seven years in the Resistance, Dirgham was hard-skinned and tough-looking. He had given Abdullah a scathing rebuke the minute he walked in.

"Drop down and give me fifty," he barked without even glancing at Abdullah. At first, Abdullah didn't think Dirgham was addressing him. But when he surveyed the room, his comrades were all staring at him and gesturing for him to get down. "And after you finish, I'm going to give that head of yours a clean shave."

Abdullah froze in place. Who the hell did this guy think he was, talking to him like that? He considered turning around and walking out. But Abdullah knew that if he did, it would be over. He'd never get a chance to pursue his military passion. And this wasn't the first day of kindergarten.

He resolved to deal with this shit stoically, throwing his satchel to the floor and going right into doing push-ups. The first thirty were pretty easy, then he began grinding his teeth. At fifty, he collapsed, but his contempt and rage outweighed his exhaustion. Dirgham was already buzzing his electric clippers near Abdullah's ear. His shiny brown hair fell in every direction as Dirgham wielded the shears in delight. After he caught his breath, Abdullah pulled a cap out of his bag and didn't remove it until his hair grew back. He was never late again. In fact, he always got to work early, and ironically, Dirgham assigned him the task of punishing latecomers.

A male voice interrupted Abdullah's thoughts. He turned to find the club president, Othman, who had invited him to the meeting. "Hey, Abdullah. *Keef halak?*"

Abdullah extended his hand and smiled. "Alhamdulillah. I thought I should come early."

They made small talk, but Abdullah, who hated delays, was eager to begin the meeting. "When do we start?" he asked Othman.

Othman gestured towards the empty seats. "When the people arrive," he said matter-of-factly, as if it were the norm. It was.

But Abdullah wouldn't let others change his habit of punctuality or waste his time. He needed to make that clear from the outset. "I hope we can start soon," Abdullah said, glancing at his watch.

Othman retrieved his phone and began calling the others. He arranged the chairs in a circle. It was 4:30 when everyone was seated. The meeting began with Othman introducing himself and asking the others to do the same.

"I'm Othman Safi," he told the group. "I work as a part-time lecturer of the Arabic language at al-Quds University, and I'm a columnist for *al-Noor Online.*"

He mentioned some of his most notable articles, the latest being *The Struggles of Arab Identity*. He then gave a summary, delving into the loss of Arab identity following the British, French, and Italian occupations. "Palestine had it the worst," he concluded. "Still occupied till this day, we're at a stalemate. The fragmentation among us Arabs is real."

Abdullah knew that these kinds of conversations led to a dead end. They were just food for thought—nothing more. But he felt the need to respond.

"It's only natural for all these drastic events to affect us in many ways. But one thing is for sure, they haven't weakened our resolve," he said as eyes shifted to him. "I'm Abdullah Mansour. You can also call me Abu Omar. I'm a freelancer for a few online newspapers, but I write mostly for *al-Araby*. My stories often focus on Palestinians in the Gaza Strip. I try to depict both the harsh reality we live under and the beautiful side of things, too."

He stopped there, offering nothing more.

For a moment, he wanted to tell them stories about his comrade Omar. About watch duty on starry nights. About all the precious moments he missed. About what it means to love your land and struggle to reclaim it. But just because these people were writers didn't mean they would be his friends.

Abdullah knew he could never really open up to people about his life. Truth be told, he'd never had a truly close companion except for Omar. It had been eight years since Omar was martyred during Operation Priceless Prey, when he was shot by an enemy sniper while bravely raiding an Israeli military base.

Othman outlined the club's purpose. They were going to establish Writers of Gaza to write and publish stories about Palestine. The club aimed to grow by recruiting new members over time. The founding writers would lead training sessions for newbies, helping them develop their craft and find their voice. They all envisioned Writers of Gaza eventually evolving into something bigger and more influential.

Today, however, they needed to assign roles and establish structure. During the first three months, the current members would meet weekly to propose story ideas, share their writing, and discuss one selected work each week. Members would rotate leading discussion circles.

When they finished, Othman invited them for coffee, tea, and refreshments. "There's Nescafé and tea. We're planning to get a coffee maker so you can enjoy American coffee."

"For me, it's only qahwa. Our qahwa," one member said with exaggerated vehemence, then chuckled.

Abdullah mingled half-heartedly. In his peripheral vision, he sensed someone watching him as two men approached. They introduced themselves as Yasin and Zuhair. Both were of medium height and lanky. Yasin had a goatee and dark circles under his eyes; a smoker, Abdullah could easily tell. Zuhair was clean-shaven, but his hair stood up a few inches. His long, pale face bore the marks of sleepless nights and undernourishment. They questioned Abdullah.

"Do you have another job besides writing? Writing can't really be considered a job unless you're a famous author," Yasin said.

Abdullah didn't flinch. "I give courses here and there, and I'm a content writer." All of it was vague, and only some of it was true.

As they talked, two women who introduced themselves as Dalia and Nuha joined them. Dalia was in her late twenties, and Nuha, despite her heavy features and thick makeup, couldn't have been more than twenty-five. They greeted the men, who seemed interested. Zuhair broke the ice with a lame question. "Who do you think are better writers, men or women?"

The younger-looking woman giggled, but Dalia said, "We'll have to see." She didn't smile or laugh, her features unreadable.

Dalia and Nuha collected members' phone numbers to create a group chat. Every so often, Abdullah could feel Dalia watching him. He filled in the necessary details and excused himself. As he was leaving, Dalia called out, "I'm going to create the group and add everyone." Abdullah glanced over his shoulder. "Okay. Thank you," he said.

Only a few minutes passed before Abdullah saw two notifications on his phone: one added him to the Writers of Gaza group chat, and the other came from an unfamiliar number. He opened that one first.

Hi, it's Dalia. I'm excited about this club! It was nice meeting you today.

Abdullah deleted the message and went home.

Chapter 4

Abdullah: The Neighbor

From a distance, Abdullah spotted Habiba in the street, watching the other kids. A group was playing hide-and-seek, and she tracked them from where she stood as they settled into their hiding spots. Her dazzling green eyes flickered with excitement, flitting from child to child as she took in every detail of the game. She'd asked Abdullah a few times if she could join in, but he'd said no.

At nine years old, Habiba had grown into a miniature beauty. She was still a child, but signs of her physical growth were becoming evident. Her face was round and full, not chubby, and her hair fell just above her shoulders.

Abdullah loved long hair, but Fatina objected to letting their daughter grow hers out. With a classroom of forty-two students, she thought it was safer and cleaner for Habiba's hair to be short. In the same way, Fatina's own mother never allowed her to grow her hair when she was in elementary school. "The *qamil* will attack your hair," she'd threatened.

"Hey, baby girl," Abdullah said when he reached his daughter. "What are you doing here? Come on inside."

Habiba followed her dad into the house, whining, "Baba, it's not fair. How come the boys get to play in the street?"

Abdullah stopped at his mother's first-floor apartment. Um Abdullah was sitting in the living room, reading from the Quran. He kissed her forehead. "Asalamu alaikum. Tata, this naughty girl wants to go out and play in the street," Abdullah said in an accusatory tone as he sat down.

Um Abdullah gasped. "Habiba! Girls don't play in the street. There are bad people out there."

Habiba's big eyes welled up, and before long, tears dripped off her chin. Abdullah sat her on his knee. "Come on, habibti, stop crying. I'll take you and Omar to the park this weekend. How does that sound?"

His daughter wrapped her arms around Abdullah's neck and rested against him. "I don't have anyone to play with. Can we go to Khaltu Amal's?"

Abdullah kissed Habiba before replying, "You can go with Mama or Tata any time."

As soon as Habiba went upstairs to their apartment, Um Abdullah spoke in a hushed voice. "Today, one of the neighbors came over. Her name is Um Masood. I unexpectedly found her standing at the main door."

"Yumma, I told you to keep that door locked."

"I did, but Habiba was outside and let her in," Um Abdullah said, calmly placing her hands in her lap.

Abdullah sighed. "So, what about this woman?"

"I could tell she came around to snoop. It seems like she's new here and pretended she just wanted to sit and chat. But then she started asking invasive questions."

Abdullah leaned forward and looked at his mother. If there was one thing he hated about people in his neighborhood, it was their lack of respect for privacy. Everyone boasted about being a close-knit community, but that meant everybody knew everybody. People poked their noses into each other's business.

He remembered how, when his sister got engaged, women would

come over and ask his mother personal questions: "How much was her dowry?" "Does the groom have a job?" "Is she going to live with her mother-in-law?"

"What did Um Masood want to know?" Abdullah asked.

Um Abdullah lowered her voice even more and peered around, as if the walls had ears. "She asked me about you. She said, 'Oh, my son Masood says Abdullah works late nights. He saw him coming home around Fajr the other day. May Allah protect him.' I tried to hide my anxiety. All I could say was that you must've gone to see your ailing aunt at the hospital and needed to get home early for work."

Abdullah's shoulders stiffened as he wondered whether this Masood was following him or was just another nosy neighbor. He needed to find out what the man and his mother were hiding.

"Yumma, I'm going to make sure this door stays locked from now on, even if I have to bolt it. As for Habiba's recklessness, I'll handle it myself." He got up to leave. When he reached the door, he turned back and said, "Oh, and that Um Masood? Don't ever let her in again."

When Abdullah reached his apartment, Habiba was playing with Omar. She had her stuffed animals and dolls lined up on the carpet, pretending to be their teacher. Seven-year-old Omar wasn't too amused. "You get to be the teacher all the time. I'm not playing with you anymore." Habiba pointed to the small board she was standing at. "I told you, you're the math teacher and I'm the Arabic teacher. They have Arabic class first. See?"

Abdullah walked in during Omar's protest. When the boy saw his dad, he ran over and hugged his legs. Abdullah picked him up and planted a kiss on his soft, chubby cheek. "You're getting bigger." Setting Omar down, he asked, "Where's Mama?"

"She's at your desk," Habiba called out.

Fatina was leafing through one of Abdullah's notebooks. When she saw him, she looked up and smiled. "I thought I should educate myself more so I can join the writers' club," she said, sheepishly.

After hearing his mother's story, Abdullah temporarily forgot about the club. He gritted his teeth, replaying Um Abdullah's words in his mind. His unease hardened into frustration.

"Maybe you should educate yourself on how to deal with Habiba!" Abdullah vented, flinging his hands onto his hips and raising his voice. "Can I ask why she goes out into the street? She's hardly a child anymore, and I don't want my children playing in the street with Allah knows who and being asked questions by nosy neighbors."

Fatina rolled her eyes. "I used to tag along with my brothers wherever they went. They never told me to go home."

Abdullah groaned and turned his head to the side, his jaw tightening. "Fine. I'll make sure she understands."

Fatina sprang up to shield their daughter from his anger.

"Habiba, your tata was upset with you because you let in a strange woman," Abdullah said loudly.

The little girl's eyes darted between her parents, and she bit her lower lip. "But the woman said she knew Tata. She asked me, 'Is your tata Um Abdullah?' and I said yes." Habiba rattled on, thinking the more she said, the more it would save her. "She also knows you and asked me where you work. I told her you're a teacher and sometimes a policeman."

Abdullah exhaled. If his life were normal, his daughter could proudly say that her father served in the army. He decided it was best to leave the room. "Mama is going to teach you about strangers again, and I don't ever want to see you standing outside," he said as he walked out.

***

It was daybreak when Abdullah returned from the mosque after Fajr prayer. He had lingered after prayers to meet one of his men, Bilal, who owned a small convenience store down the street, across from the mosque. Despite there being a supermarket in the same neighborhood, Bilal still had a good number of customers, especially schoolchildren.

One good thing about owning a store in a densely populated area was getting to know the residents. Storeowners often sat outside their shops, talking and observing passersby. Every day was nearly the same, unless there was an attack. But even during military escalations, many stores stayed open, having faith that they weren't targets.

Abdullah waited until the mosque was mostly empty of worshipers to approach Bilal. A few men sat reading the Quran. The two shook hands and settled on the carpet, away from the others. Abdullah had known Bilal since university. He was an intelligence officer—their eyes in the neighborhood.

"I need to know everything you can find out about Masood and everyone who lives in that house. Have you met any of them?"

Each held a Quran, pretending to discuss verses.

"They moved here only three months ago. I'm not sure how many people live in the house, but I've seen a middle-aged man, a young woman—possibly his wife—who covers her face, and an elderly woman. There are also two kids. The old woman seems to lead a very social life since moving here. The man doesn't seem to have a day job. He goes out at about 2:00 p.m. and returns late at night." Bilal tried to remember if there was anything else worth mentioning.

The information was too general for Abdullah. "Do they have visitors?"

"I've never noticed, but they go out often, especially the young woman."

"Bilal, I need you to assign three of our men to follow them—one for each person. Tell them to start tomorrow. Report to me next Thursday, just before Dhuhr prayer. And listen, get Salem for the job."

"Insha'Allah."

Bilal got up, put the Quran on a nearby shelf, and left. Abdullah stayed at the mosque for another ten minutes before heading home.

Chapter 5

Abdullah: An Idea

TWO DAYS HAD PASSED since the writers' club meeting when Othman called Abdullah. "Do you want to grab a coffee this afternoon?" he asked.

Abdullah made a mental check of his schedule. He had a workout at 3:00, a part of his routine that was set in stone. "I can make it around 5:00. Is that good?"

"Okay. It'll just be the two of us. Let's meet at Aroma Café by the beach. You know the place?"

"I won't get lost in Gaza."

The entire Gaza Strip was very small—a tiny dot on the map, covering only 141 square miles. People who spent their whole lives there were accustomed to short distances and quick travel times. It often made Abdullah wonder how vast the outside world was and whether he had the capacity to grasp its sweeping expanses. He wouldn't know until he experienced it.

Abdullah finished his workout at the gym, jogged home, showered, and put on casual blue jeans and a white T-shirt. His state of mind often inspired his clothing choices. But sometimes it was the other way around; he'd wear light colors to cheer himself up.

Restaurants, wedding halls, and cafés lined the beachfront, their outdoor tables extending toward the sea, with wooden swing benches swaying gently in some spots. Boys as young as seven went from table to table, selling sunflower seeds or cheap candy bars. In reality, it was another form of begging, as they'd nag people into buying something.

Abdullah spotted Aroma Café quickly. It sat on an elevated corner across from the beach. A large screen showed a football match, and a group of young men were glued to it as they smoked hookah and sipped hot drinks. He scanned the faces. Othman wasn't there yet.

He couldn't see himself sitting inside amid the noise and commotion. Abdullah's routine with Fatina was to get away from the crowds whenever possible and enjoy solitude. It was a habit that suited his contemplative writer self.

"Hey, Abdullah." Othman popped in from behind him.

Medium in height and broad-shouldered, Othman's eyes were deep-set, and his hair was parted on one side in the popular style. He wore khaki pants and a navy button-down shirt. Abdullah guessed the guy was a formal type. This was their second encounter, and Abdullah had a good impression of him—intelligent and serious.

Othman studied him. "You seem like someone who can't afford to lose a minute."

"I like to stick to a schedule. It helps me get more done."

They ordered coffee and cake. Spring was around the corner, and while the biting cold was gone, the late-afternoon breeze remained chilly. Abdullah pulled his jacket more snugly around his shoulders. If Fatina were sitting beside him now, she'd be clinging to him for warmth, a thought that brought a soft fire to his chest.

Suddenly, his phone blinked. *Hey, handsome, I'm near our rock. Meet me there.* Abdullah tried to hide his smile, but he was too excited. Telepathy!

Othman paused mid-sentence when he noticed Abdullah was distracted.

"Please, go on," Abdullah urged. He thought about how Othman would never be someone he could confide romantic secrets to.

"I've read most of your articles, Abdullah, defending the Resistance. Your latest piece is quite intriguing. *The Balaclava Heroes*, right?"

"Yes," Abdullah said, nodding. "My brother was martyred during the Second Intifada. And I've lost a few friends, too. I have to honor their legacy, even if only through writing. People don't know the struggles of the freedom fighters, and I think I can help readers understand them in a way that makes them connect."

Othman listened attentively, and Abdullah could tell he was holding back another question. "I know there's consensus here on the effectiveness of Resistance. The majority support it, especially after the latest Israeli aggression. But you know how we're portrayed in the international media," Othman said.

Abdullah was still trying to figure out where Othman was going. "Yeah, we're called terrorists, as usual."

"The thing is that no matter how hard we try to change this image, the media still twists the facts and doesn't give the Palestinian narrative a fair chance," Othman continued. "That's what I want to discuss with you. Recently, I met with a youth group to discuss new forms of resistance—popular resistance. We plan to meet with NGOs, political factions, academics, and social figures. We want to organize a massive protest on Palestinian Land Day."

Growing up, Abdullah often heard about peace talks and negotiations, but as far as he knew, they amounted to nothing, and they certainly hadn't stopped the Israelis from killing his people. Childhood memories of Israeli occupation attacks had been seared into his mind. They had been ongoing for as long as he could remember. But this massive protest idea was innovative, and he was willing to see if it might pave the way for other forms of resistance.

Othman laid out the proposed course of action. "People from all over the Gaza Strip will mobilize near the separation fence, en masse. Whole families will be there, not only men. We're planning to meet next week to discuss the details, and I thought you'd like to be part of this."

Abdullah's interest was piqued. "I'll be there."

With that, he parted ways with Othman and made his way down to the beach to meet Fatina.

Chapter 6

Fatina: The Rock

A ROW OF BRIGHTLY-COLORED CONCRETE BENCHES lined the street overlooking the beach. Fatina loved the ample space between them that allowed for privacy. The spot also had a spectacular panoramic view.

In the near-spring evenings, people were starting to venture out. On the shore, vendors with horse-drawn carts sold balloons in all sorts of shapes and colors. A camel handler offered rides for five shekels. The camel was adorned with colorful tassels and two wool pouches. Tents for rent were scattered across the sand for those who preferred them. But many opted for a table with chairs and an umbrella, especially for short visits.

The swishing of the waves formed a distant, tranquil symphony. It reminded Fatina of all the places she couldn't reach, like tropical islands where the waves would tickle her feet as she sat, toying with seashells. Running her fingers over them, feeling their varied textures and examining their patterns, she just knew she'd feel an inexplicable affinity for them—not just for the ordinary clam-shaped shells, but also for the more intricate spirals. She would find a shell, put it to her ear, and discover new sounds. Maybe seashells had their own world, and by washing ashore, they were allowing humans a glimpse into the unknown, she thought.

The waters would be a calming, crystal blue, unlike the greenish-gray sea she watched now.

Abdullah's playful teasing cut her thoughts short. "Waiting for your man, fair lady?"

Fatina's heart leapt. Her husband's voice had an instantly soothing effect. It made everything feel alright, even when things weren't.

"You saw my message this time!"

"At the same time as I was thinking about you."

Jumping up, Fatina hugged Abdullah's arm, and they strolled through the sand, its coarse granules filling their shoes. They sat on their rock, happy to see their special spot still there, which brought back fond memories of their early days together. Abdullah pulled Fatina close, and they held each other.

"This is the perfect place to celebrate, isn't it?" Abdullah turned to Fatina. "Happy anniversary, habibti," he whispered in her ear. Fatina's eyes glistened with tears, and she buried her face in Abdullah's arm.

The crashing waves grew louder, the air damp with salt. This was the feeling Fatina cherished. Suddenly, everything felt whole again. Her worries were lighter, her broken pieces mended, her downtrodden soul lifted. If only things could stay this way.

Chapter 7

Abdullah: The Great March of Return

"The idea is to organize a peaceful protest on March 30, Land Day. It will be the first of its kind. There will be five encampment areas across the Gaza Strip near the separation fence. People will be bused from city centers to the designated areas. They will sit 500 to 700 meters from the fence to avoid friction with Israeli soldiers. There will be folk singing and other performances."

Othman had just laid out the plan for the massive protest to the committee, which consisted of twenty-odd people from various civil society organizations and political factions. It included both tribal and public figures.

Abdullah edged his chair forward, keeping his eyes on Othman, just like everyone else. Only the fan hummed in the background.

A senior member—a man whose wrinkles seemed to shift up and down with involuntary twitches—was twisting his mustache. Abdullah could tell this man was a first-generation refugee. Next to him sat another older member, whose age Abdullah guessed to be in the late fifties. He didn't see the man's face, but his strong cologne reminded him of an old university professor who used to wear oil-based perfumes people brought back from Hajj. Scanning the crowd of younger attendees, Abdullah saw that they were all sitting silently, just as apprehensive as he was.

"Would this be a one-day protest? And if so, how would that get the message across?" Abdullah asked.

An elderly member from the Union of Trades spoke. He had a round face with patches of red from one side to the other, as if an electric blanket were under his skin. "The plan is to make it weekly until the commemoration of the Nakba. That means it will run for about a month and a half, starting on March 30."

A member from the Ministry of Culture added, "We'll keep protesting until we eventually move near the fence. On that day, the protestors will all hold hands and approach it. We will demand our right to return to our land." His nostrils flared.

They were making it sound so easy—as if the soldiers would just let the people in. Of course, that wouldn't happen. The Israeli army would shoot. They had done it before, and they'd do it again. Abdullah dug his nails into his forearm to keep from snapping at the minister. Instead, he laced his fingers on the table and let the silence stretch before speaking.

"I don't mean to undermine this plan, but…do you actually think it's realistic? I mean, just imagine crowds moving toward the fence. Chances are, the soldiers will react violently," he said, his gaze shifting to the people across the room. "We're not talking about a workers' or a teachers' strike. This is a large-scale civil movement protesting the occupation of our lands. Do you think we can just return to our lands so effortlessly by holding hands and chanting for freedom?"

Some members nodded in all-too-obvious silent agreement. A more enthusiastic member raised his voice to counter. "We will never know unless we try! By international law, we have the right to assemble peacefully. We'll get media coverage, and the whole world will be watching. Do you think the Israelis will commit a massacre in front of the TV cameras?"

They've done it before, Abdullah thought.

A voice burst out, "We haven't forgotten what happened to Mohammed al-Durra."

The videotaped slaughter of Mohammed was seared into every Palestinian's memory. Abdullah remembered how horrifying it was to see a child cowering behind his father for safety, only to be shot and killed.

The impassioned conversation energized a woman from the Popular Front. Her brows were in a permanent furrow, and her lips curled in scorn. She followed suit, raising her voice louder than the previous speaker's and banging her fist on the table.

"We can make this happen! We must show the world that we're peaceful and that we can regain our rights by calling for them through peaceful means. The international media portrays us as terrorists who relish violence. They will see that we're just ordinary people. This doesn't make us weak. No. Peaceful assembly validates our call for justice and freedom!"

The atmosphere was already beginning to resemble a zealous protest.

Abdullah truly wanted to believe it would work, that he and his family would join hands and reclaim the city they had been forcibly displaced from. To him, the goal was justified, but the means felt fanciful. The image of peaceful protesters holding hands had never worked in any struggle for freedom. It only seemed suitable for purely civic reasons, like protesting the demolition of a historic building, or for things he saw in movies.

But Abdullah wasn't pigheaded. Maybe if everyone believed it could work, he should stop being skeptical. After all, the majority of the committee members were veterans with more life experience than he had.

The meeting ended, and everyone was to prepare for the Great March of Return.

Chapter 8

Abdullah: Information

ON HIS WAY OUT of the March of Return meeting, Abdullah's phone rang. It was Bilal. Sounding bored, he complained that his day was as uneventful as usual. It was impossible to pass on any sensitive information over the phone. "I hope I didn't catch you at a bad time," Bilal said.

"I'm on my way home," Abdullah replied.

"I wouldn't want to cause a fuss with Um Omar, but I just got some freshly ground coffee. You should come try it."

"I'm on my way. Save me a pack for Um Omar. Coffee appeases her."

Abdullah had been anticipating the information about his dubious neighbors. His team had been observing them, and he needed to know what Bilal had found out.

That day, Abdullah hadn't taken his car. In fact, when the weather was fair and he wasn't in a hurry, he preferred to get around by walking. He walked down Nasser Street, where his favorite coffee shop, Costa, was located. People had a penchant for choosing foreign names for restaurants, pharmacies, supermarkets, and even auto parts shops. They thought it gave their businesses prestige.

It would take Abdullah at least fifteen minutes to get to Bilal's, but he didn't mind. Bilal was at his store and wouldn't be going anywhere. The walk would give him time to reflect on what happened at the writers' meeting. For starters, that woman, Dalia, hardly struck him as a writer. Not that he pictured a writer looking a certain way, but she lacked the depth typically associated with one.

Hands in his pockets, he continued along Nasser Street. With only two lanes on each side and cars parked along the curb, there was little space left for traffic to pass. Shops, residences, and commercial buildings stood on both sides of the street, imposing a heavy presence with their concrete structures.

Vegetable sellers riding mule-drawn carts called out, "Eggplants, onions, potatoes, zucchini! Five shekels for a kilo of cucumbers!" Cars honked, engines backfired, sirens wailed, and a sea of commuters flooded the streets. Abdullah covered his nose with his scarf to block the choking exhaust fumes from a motorcycle as it sped past.

Everything was relentlessly alive.

It was midday, with about twenty minutes to go before the noon prayer, Dhuhr. At this hour, the morning shift at the overcrowded United Nations Relief and Works Agency all-boys school was letting out, part of the double-shift system that ran morning and afternoon classes. Raucous shouts reverberated from inside as Abdullah passed by. He quickened his step, but he was too late. The school gate swung open, and he was almost knocked off his feet as small boys in blue jeans and T-shirts stampeded out.

Abdullah stopped. Turning to observe the scene, his heart warmed. The boys were so vibrant with energy, running out of school as if it were the start of a holiday. But still, many of them lingered near the gates before eventually making their way home.

A group had marbles. They sat on the sidewalk, and each boy showed off his collection. Abdullah could hear the clacking as little fingers flicked the marbles across the pavement. The thumping of shoes caught his attention as another group bolted to the ice cream stall, their backpacks flopping about. Others were either chasing, racing, or just running in different directions, emitting shrills and calls.

Abdullah remembered that feeling from childhood. Once, he was just like those kids. In retrospect, childhood was the only form of freedom he'd ever known. It was a time when his life revolved around eating and playing, and nothing else seemed to matter or even exist. These kids had that same carefree energy. He wished he could give them a collective hug and protect them from occupation and war. He silently prayed for them and moved on.

A handful of school kids were buying snacks when Abdullah reached Bilal's store. A boy had a shekel and slid it across the counter. He bought potato chips and a chocolate bar. Practically glowing with excitement, he clutched the snacks as if they were treasures.

"I keep telling you, Bilal, why don't you start selling carrots and bananas to these poor kids? See how anemic they look?" Abdullah said listlessly. He knew it was useless. Nobody was competing for high standards in customer service here. Kids would keep coming in to buy junk food, and nothing would change.

"I'd have to turn it into a grocery store then. I wouldn't mind, but you think these kids can afford fruit?"

Abdullah silently scolded himself for caring too much. He brought a plastic chair over to the counter and asked, "So, what do you have for me?"

Bilal waited until the last kids scuttled out of the store. "My man followed the woman we think is Masood's wife out of her house and saw her enter a building on Jalal Street. She was fully covered in her abaya and niqab when she went into the building. He didn't see which floor she went up to."

Abdullah's eyes grew larger, and he rested his elbows on the table. "Did you say a building on Jalal Street?"

"Yup. Al-Safa building."

"That's the place I go for my weekly writers' meeting. It's on the seventh floor." Abdullah's mind raced back to Dalia and Nuha, the two female group members who tried to engage with him. "Did he see her when she left?"

"Yes, but she didn't come down till 9:30. There's no institute in that building that stays open that late. There was a man with her. My guy got a photo of them, but it was dark, and the man's face was lost in shadows."

"Listen, we have to bug the seventh floor. I have an uneasy feeling about a woman at my writers' club. This is the only way to track her movements," Abdullah said.

Bilal folded his arms and leaned back. "I have to figure out how we're going to install a camera."

"We need to work from inside the unit," Abdullah said. "There's a small study room. Let's get in there and set everything up, but first I'll do a sweep to make sure the place isn't already bugged."

Technology wasn't Abdullah's strong suit, so he'd get professional help.

Chapter 9

Salem: Pursuit

ONCE AGAIN, the meeting ended, but Dalia didn't come down for another two hours.

Salem was Bilal's undercover agent. Impersonating a languid college student, he had just attended his first writers' meeting under the pretense of being interested in the club. A clean shave and an absurd amount of gel—enough to make his hair glow—completed the look.

When asked why he wanted to join the club, Salem said, "I believe it can help me improve my writing skills, which I need for my university assignments, and hopefully it'll help me start my own blog." After a few more standard questions, Othman admitted him, leaving Salem free to begin his real task of following Dalia.

After everyone left, Salem lingered a bit between the aisles, browsing the books. Then, as Dalia and Nuha were leaving, he followed. The meeting room was on the seventh floor, but they chose the stairs. He started after them, waiting until they disappeared behind the first landing. He listened for the click of shoes to see if they'd stopped descending.

A door opened.

Salem dashed down but didn't catch which door they entered. He couldn't risk staying any longer in case there were cameras, so he took the elevator to the ground level.

At the building's entrance, a caretaker sat at a battered table. Salem cringed at the cheap reception decor. He asked the caretaker, "Is Media Town Company's office on the sixth floor?"

The caretaker, a man in his late forties, paid little attention as he scrolled through his phone. "The sixth? No, the sixth only has private apartments," he said without looking up.

This was too easy for Salem. There was an advantage to appointing half-witted caretakers for buildings after all.

"Media Town is on the fourth," the man continued. Still scrolling, he pointed to the large tenant directory listing the names of offices and residences in the building.

Salem thanked him and walked out. He waited behind a car until 9:30 and saw two women, fully covered from head to toe, leave the building. He couldn't remember seeing them, but it didn't take long to spot a giveaway. One of them had the same bag Dalia carried.

During the writers' meeting, he'd analyzed Dalia and Nuha's clothing, handbags, shoes, accessories, and hijabs. Nuha dressed garishly. Everything she wore either glittered or glowed. Dalia's taste was more refined, yet subtly seductive for a woman in their society. Even the way she wore her hijab seemed intended to reveal more than to cover.

They walked down an alley before getting into a white, beat-up 2005 Skoda Octavia. Salem quickly noted the license plate number. He slipped a black hoodie over his shoulders, tugged his helmet into place, mounted the motorcycle, and pursued the old car.

Chapter 10

Abdullah: Reading Session

ABDULLAH RAN HIS FINGERS along the books on the shelves in the library's history section. The way he had to tilt his head to see the titles annoyed him. Why did they have to be placed vertically? Horizontal shelving would be much easier on the eyes. He'd never seen a library with horizontally shelved books, but that didn't matter to him. Just because everybody did something a certain way didn't mean it was the only way. He'd discovered many things people did that he found utter nonsense, like binge-shopping a day before Ramadan.

Picking up a book on the rise and fall of the Ottoman Empire, he moved to a nearby table to read until it was time for the meeting. Although Abdullah had never liked history in school, he recently became interested in reading about the rise and fall of nations. Living in a highly politicized place, he had learned firsthand about his country's history. But now he wanted to study other nations that the world's great powers had colonized.

Abdullah was early as usual, but the moment two figures appeared in his peripheral vision, he regretted his punctuality.

"*Marhaba*, Abdullah. Sorry to interrupt your reading." It was Dalia.

Abdullah didn't register remorse in her voice.

He responded with a curt *"Marhaba"* without looking up. It wasn't welcoming, but he didn't care. From the corner of his vision, he saw the two women glance at one another as if to signal the next move.

"We wanted to ask about one of your published stories, *The Balaclava Heroes*. It's a brilliant piece. How did you get the idea for it?" Nuha asked with exaggerated interest, her eyes bulging with theatrical excitement.

Abdullah wasn't used to being this close to unfamiliar women. His job didn't involve women, and he'd never been with any woman except Fatina. She was his first and only love. He liked to relive the day he met her at the stationery shop.

Even with his gaze lowered, he could feel their stares penetrating him. He didn't invite them to sit. "I'm planning to discuss this during today's session, so I'll answer your question there."

He was saved by Othman, who sauntered in at just the right moment. Getting up, Abdullah left the book on the table and the two women standing there.

The tables and chairs were arranged in a circle, ready for the meeting to start. As they all sat down, Dalia checked her makeup in her pocket mirror. She touched up her red lipstick. It shimmered on her protruding lips, giving her an air of arrogance.

He wasn't sure whether it was plastic surgery or just lipstick that caused her lips to stick out. He had overheard his sister and wife discussing plastic surgery one day, something uncommon in Gaza. It was probably the lipstick itself. She wore black skinny jeans and a long white cardigan over a flaring red shirt—tight enough for everyone to see what was underneath.

Othman opened the session by welcoming the newest member, Salem. The topic for discussion was Abdullah's *The Balaclava Heroes*. Having read it, Othman recommended it to the members. One of the women distributed copies of the story.

Abdullah waited until everyone was seated, then said, "I invited a guest without consulting the group, and she should be here about now. I hope you don't mind." He tried to suppress his smile.

The group looked up at the ajar door. There was a knock, then someone gently pushed it open.

It was Fatina.

Abdullah stepped forward to usher her in. Ever since the night he came home angry, he felt he owed it to her to show her that he wanted her to be part of his world. He led her to the circle. Fatina's cheeks flushed. She wasn't accustomed to being the center of attention, especially with men present.

"Everybody, I'd like you to meet my lovely wife, Fatina. Um Omar."

Fatina didn't make eye contact with anyone. She squeezed Abdullah's hand hard, not letting go, then greeted everyone with a barely audible "asalamu alaikum" before sitting beside her husband.

When Abdullah invited her, she had nearly gawked at him and asked, "There will be men there, right?" Abdullah had chuckled at her remark. "I know everyone is going to see my gorgeous wife, but that doesn't mean they'll kidnap you," he said.

Now, Abdullah sat quietly. He didn't want to see them staring at Fatina, so he shuffled the papers in front of him.

"*Ahlan wa sahlan*," Othman said warmly. "Welcome to our group. Are you a writer yourself, Um Omar?"

Fatina looked at Abdullah and smiled. "I can't say I'm a writer, but I love to read good writing."

"In other words, you're a reader. Welcome to the club."

Chapter 11

Abdullah: The Balaclava Heroes

ABDULLAH READ from his notebook, his hands shaking as he turned the pages.

The Balaclava Heroes

"It's a shame that other people can't see your beautiful face," she said softly, tracing his lips with her index finger. "I'd be proud if you could walk down the street in your military uniform and have people shower you with roses."

He kissed her fingertip gently, holding their gaze. "I can live with being an anonymous soldier if that's my destiny. I'm content knowing I'm your hero." He pulled her close to him.

They sat on the bench, holding each other like ships docking at port. They could be frozen in time and would ask for nothing more.

Why did it hurt to be in love? Wasn't it something every person fights and struggles for—to love and be loved, to find someone who completes the missing pieces, who takes you by the hand and reassures you of their presence? It hurts to love because love in this world is mortal. It hurts because there's an end to every journey, an end to every moment, whether happy or sad. Just as the sun sinks into the horizon when we wish it would stay a moment longer—gradually bidding us farewell, leaving us with an empty feeling, reminding us of the goodbyes we so often make—so too does love slip away.

When two lovers unite, they believe nothing can separate them. But complex reality pulls them apart, and the moment comes to an end. No matter how fulfilled they feel, it's all momentary, and they're left with a void inside.

She wasn't content with his answer. She wished her hero could be free to reveal his face to his people, to come and go without having to keep his duty secret. She wanted to see him honored at ceremonies and awarded new titles and badges before large audiences that would applaud his valor. But instead, he operated in anonymity, forced to wear a balaclava that barely revealed his eyes. Those eyes, fierce and powerful behind the mask, turned tender when they met hers.

"People outside associate you with terrorists and murderers when they see the face covering. It's unfair. This balaclava doesn't do you justice. You should be wearing a military cap with your uniform, like soldiers elsewhere."

He could sense the turmoil radiating from her body to his. He gently rubbed her arm, drawing her closer again. "There will come a day when my comrades and I will walk our streets freely. But for now, will you be content that I'm your hero?"

Throughout, Abdullah's tone was somber, and its effect was clear on everyone present. When he finished, silence settled over the room, broken only by the ticking of an old wall clock. Twenty-four pairs of eyes darted between him and Fatina. He turned and found her dabbing at her tear-stained cheeks with a tissue.

"Your story is touching, Abdullah… you can clearly see its impact," Othman said, trying to brighten the atmosphere.

Abdullah rearranged the papers in front of him over and over. "I didn't realize I was such a tragic writer."

Some of the attendees laughed, but the mood remained melancholy. He tried to explain Fatina's emotional reaction before anyone caught on. "She's… it must've reminded her of a friend who was martyred a few years back. He was special. Omar."

It was still so silent that Abdullah could hear people adjusting in their chairs. Finally, one of the men spoke. "It reminded me of my cousin. He was killed during the Intifada." Another followed suit: "My neighbor, too." He didn't feel the need to say much more.

As collective empathy filled the room, Abdullah commiserated, "May Allah have mercy on their souls."

Everyone in Gaza had either lost a loved one in Israeli attacks or knew someone who had.

Othman intervened. "I'm sorry for your losses. It seems Abdullah's piece has brought up memories for many of us. Let's begin with questions or feedback." He glanced at Abdullah, who was distracted. "Or better yet, maybe we can do that after a short break."

When he finished speaking, Fatina immediately excused herself.

Abdullah placed the papers on the table and also pushed back his chair. His plan was to make Fatina happy by inviting her to the session. He hadn't expected her to break down when he read his story. But he knew it stirred more than memories of Omar and the other martyrs. It tugged at something deeper, a well of grief Fatina carried within herself.

Now and then, Fatina would have an episode of sadness when buried memories resurfaced. She'd tell Abdullah it was a temporary phase, but he disagreed. He even tried to convince her that therapy sessions would help, but she refused.

Following his wife out of the library, he found her in the small study room.

"I'm sorry, I…" She covered her mouth, no longer able to hold back her emotions. Clutching Abdullah's shirt, she struggled to control her sobs.

"It's okay, baby. Was my story that bad?" Abdullah stroked Fatina's back.

Trying to calm down, she softly replied, "Abood, your words scare me. Your story is too real."

He held both her hands and kissed them. "I'll get you a coffee. I'll try to keep the Q&A brief, and we can talk at home. Okay?"

"What are they saying about me? I've made a fool of myself." She looked up at Abdullah, her eyes moist.

"No, they're not. They're talking about the story." He brushed away her tears with his thumbs.

When Abdullah returned to the group, everyone was back in their seats and ready to ask questions. He braced himself. They'd be asking for details, but he could handle this.

One man raised his hand, and Abdullah nodded to him. "It's an amazing story, man. I admire your poetic way of bringing us into the lives of the freedom fighters. We hardly give their personal lives much thought. We don't think about how they spend nights away from home or the impact their sacrifices have on their loved ones. My question is, why do you think so many young men here are attracted to the Resistance when it's so risky?"

Abdullah was composed despite the turmoil within him. He remembered the moment he decided to join the Resistance. It came after an Israeli missile killed his brother. At the time, his sense of vengeance was strong, and it only grew more intense as the number of martyrs kept increasing.

The word "risky" triggered memories of his comrade, Ahmed, who died in the tunnels. There were no safety measures at the time. In retrospect, Abdullah realized that eight years ago, the tunnel work was primitive compared with today.

"Based on the stories I hear, simply put, they want freedom. I believe today's youth can no longer tolerate living under occupation. So, anyone who joins the Resistance is tired of pretending life is good when they see the daily havoc of the occupation on our people. They understand the power of the Resistance, are naturally drawn to it, and yearn to be part of a movement that truly seeks to achieve liberation for our homeland."

A woman raised her hand. Othman nodded for her to speak. She was young and energetic, and the topic clearly excited her. Her face lit up as she spoke. She jumbled her words, exclaiming, "I'd love to marry a freedom fighter!"

Laughter erupted from the group.

She paused briefly in surprise, then continued. "I think they're the most courageous and beautiful people. I know they put their lives on the line for us, and I'd probably worry about my husband—if I marry a freedom fighter, that is," she said, blushing. "But I think it's the noblest thing."

Then she flapped her hands in the air as if to stop herself. "Anyway, I was wondering if you could tell us something about your friend, Omar."

Abdullah was taken aback. From how she was rambling, he assumed she merely wanted to express her admiration. If he talked about Omar, he feared he'd get too personal. But he also couldn't talk about him abstractly.

"It'd take me hours to talk about Omar, but I can send you a link to an article I wrote about him if…"

"But can't you just tell us something about him, please?" she cut him off. "What was he like? How was he martyred?"

Abdullah was cornered. He exhaled, his words coming out slowly. "I believe Omar knew he would leave this world early. He dreamed of Jannah and a *houri* whom he often spoke of."

He remembered exactly when Omar first told him about the dream. It was a beautiful, starry night, and Omar hadn't taken his gaze off the sky as he spoke.

"I never told anyone until after he was martyred. Omar said that in his dream, the *houri* gave him a rifle."

The stillness of the room grew heavy.

"Then, just as she was about to vanish, he asked her name. You know how it is when you have a dream and become obsessed with it? It was like that. He was never the same after."

There was a clamor of voices.

"What was her name?"

Everyone stared intently at Abdullah.

The conversation stirred deep emotions in Abdullah. Images replayed in his mind, their details as vivid as a summer sky, and he remembered how Omar had repeatedly recounted the dream. It was a divine revelation. Abdullah's chest ached with the weight of memory.

"Her name was Hasna," he said quietly.

"Ah, so beautiful," said the girl who asked the question, her large eyes downcast and thoughtful.

The discussion could have gone on for hours, but Abdullah excused himself. He went to the study room, where Fatina was waiting. She had opened the door to listen.

"You were great," she said, smiling as her eyes glistened.

Chapter 12

Dalia: The Brother

"Anything new?" Masood furrowed his brow as he looked at Dalia.

The dim lighting cast shadows across his face. She escaped his stare by studying a dark stain on the maroon tablecloth between them. The thick, wood-paneled walls of the shawarma restaurant boxed her in. She inhaled sharply.

The mission Masood assigned to her was making her restless. It was clear that Abdullah's nature wouldn't allow him to engage in anything immoral. He wouldn't even notice her, let alone be seduced. She had to abandon this mission. She was fed up with the whole ordeal.

"Look, this man is too damn ethical and stubborn. I can't get through to him," she exhaled in defeat. The Turkish coffee she had ordered earlier was dark and still, like swamp water. She reached out, grabbed the cup by the rim, and drank it in one gulp, bitter and cold.

Masood stared her down, his eyes flashing with malice. "There's no such thing as an impregnable man. You see, my naive little sister, every man has a weakness for certain things. You know that by now, don't you?"

"Well, this one happens to be happily married," Dalia snapped, her nostrils flaring. "And his wife is attractive."

Masood glanced around to check whether anyone was close enough to hear. He had been given a month to execute this operation. It was part of a large scheme to infiltrate the Resistance and bring down the fighters. "Then we move to plan B," he said in a steady, composed tone.

"Which is?" Dalia eyed him. Her stomach turned. Her brother knew no bounds. She could expect the worst.

"Mother visited them recently, and she got into their house easily. I'm sure she can do it again." Masood studied his interlocked hands on the table. Then he let his final words land. "I'm going to have her plant a device in their home."

Dalia bristled with cold fury. She was appalled at the thought of her brother exploiting their mother.

Masood stretched his arms behind his back as if they were having the most ordinary of conversations. "I still have to report to Officer Eyad, and he's going to ask me about the developments. He'll be pissed off to hear that you've accomplished nothing. Or should I say you've failed?"

"I told you from the beginning that I'm not good at playing your dirty games. Why don't you fire me and find someone else, since I'm a complete failure?" Dalia's cheeks burned.

"Not so fast, darling. It's not that simple. I can't just swap you with another agent. There's only one way out of this game, and you know it very well." Masood's tone was menacing.

With Masood's threat hanging over her, she was weak and trapped. Thoughts of her children flickered through Dalia's mind. As for her self-worth, she felt like scum.

Dalia had shut herself off after her husband divorced her and left her with their two kids. She moved back home. Her father had passed away, so she was forced to live with her mother and her insolent brother. Masood took advantage of his vulnerable sister, implicating her in his treacherous work with the Israeli occupation.

Some of her missions involved seducing men for information. Masood had dragged her into a filthy pit, and she had become desensitized. She eventually reached a point where she no longer felt sorry for the victims because she was a victim herself, one who had been badly abused.

At first, Masood didn't clearly tell her what she was getting herself into. Instead, he asked her to do seemingly small tasks. He wanted her to find out how many people lived in this or that house or who visited this or that neighbor. All of it served his larger goal of collecting information. In return, he gave her money he received from the Israeli officer.

When Dalia realized the extent of her involvement, Masood told her there was no way out. Her name had already been passed to the officer. If she tried to quit or step out of line, they'd eliminate her without hesitation.

Chapter 13

Abdullah: A Bold Move

Abdullah wasn't attached to his phone. He couldn't take it with him during his military activities, and he didn't like being harassed by chat groups. He kept its use to a minimum. But when he got home a few hours after the reading session, there were dozens of notifications. He checked. Over ten messages from Dalia.

> *It was lovely meeting your wife. I didn't get a chance to speak with her, so maybe you can invite her again. Or better yet, she could become a member of our club.*
> *There's something I want to talk to you about…*
> *You're like a brother to me. I don't mean that you look old or anything (smiley face).*

Abdullah exhaled in exasperation.

> *It's an issue I've been hiding because I don't know who to turn to. A relative of mine harasses me.*
> *You can't imagine how I feel.*
> *I've told no one about this because it's hard for me to trust people*
> *…and you know what our society is like.*

He was incredulous. Why was this woman telling him this? Just reading it felt sinful.

> *I trust you can tell me what to do without making
> this public. I came up with a plan to get him
> caught.*
> *The next time he calls me and asks me over, I'll
> give you the address, and you can catch him in
> the act.*

Abdullah's eyes were locked on the screen.

> *But PLEASE, I don't want anyone else involved.
> You know how people here stigmatize girls, and I
> fear for my reputation.*

Abdullah didn't flinch. True, he had admirers during university and one second cousin who had been interested in him, but none had ever dared to make such a bold move. As far as he could tell, he hadn't given Dalia any indication that he was interested in even striking up a conversation with her or her goofy friend.

Living under occupation had taught him to be wary of people, to keep his relationships limited, and not to let others into his life easily. Often, Israeli intelligence agencies employed spies from the neighborhood where Abdullah lived. He remembered a time when he was a teenager and a high school girl would wait for him near his home. One day, she passed him a note. When Abdullah opened it, he couldn't believe what it said. She'd tried to seduce him. It was hard for a seventeen-year-old to resist, but he did. It turned out the girl had been hired to target young men and recruit them as potential informants for Israeli intelligence.

Given the bluntness of Dalia's message, Abdullah knew he needed help. He called Bilal.

"Hey, man. We have some homemade cake. It's fresh." That was all Abdullah needed to say.

"Put on the kettle," Bilal replied.

Fatina entered the living room. She'd just showered, and her hair was still damp. She wore a pair of dark blue skinny jeans and a red pullover. Abdullah loved how her lustrous black hair always made red look magical.

"Who did you just invite to eat my cake?" she teased, walking over to Abdullah and wrapping her arms around his neck.

He caught the scent of her jasmine-scented shampoo. "I could do my breathing exercises right here," he said, caressing her neck.

Fatina giggled. "I don't mind, but not in the middle of the house."

Abdullah knew that brief moments of intimacy were enough to comfort Fatina whenever she was down. Twelve years into their marriage, he never felt their relationship had grown stale. True, time was still on their side, but he sensed it meant more to Fatina.

Since they married, they'd gone through serious, life-changing ups and downs. The shelling, Fatina's injury, the nights and days when Abdullah was away on duty, and the martyrdom of people they loved. Fatina had experienced nervous breakdowns, during which she isolated herself by staying silent most of the time, sleeping excessively, and avoiding going out.

After the attack that maimed her hand, Abdullah supported her by taking her horseback riding. Connecting with the horse helped soothe Fatina, at least for a while. But the trauma kept resurfacing. Even a slamming door would make her jump. She had told Abdullah she was beyond repair.

Sometimes, handling the kids felt easy compared to navigating Fatina's constant anxiety. Daydreaming about a family trip—even just to nearby Egypt—he imagined giving Fatina a break from her worries. Memories of visiting as a child with his father surfaced: the zoo, the theme park, the excitement.

Bilal rang the doorbell, and Abdullah led him into the guest room.

A three-seater sofa sat along one wall, with a loveseat perpendicular to it, both upholstered in grass-green fabric and accented with floral cushions. On the other side of the room were two recliners, and in the center stood a small oak coffee table adorned with a silver plate dotted with candles. A small beige woven rug accentuated the furniture's beauty and cozy charm. It was all Fatina's way of trying to bring nature into their home with the limited means she had.

Bilal sat on the large sofa, his legs spread out. "What is it this time, Abood, marriage advice?" he teased. Abdullah knew that Bilal's jokes were a façade, hiding something more intense and fooling people into believing he was okay. But the trauma he had endured still haunted him.

Over time, Bilal had shared the story in fragments, never all at once, never without shutting down at some point.

He had fallen in love with Jasmine and spent a year hoping her parents would agree to give him her hand. They insisted she finish university first, so he counted down the days until that moment finally arrived. Now, two years had passed since Bilal's wedding, but his marriage had lasted only a month.

One summer morning, a month after their wedding, Bilal heard Jasmine faintly calling his name. He dashed to the kitchen and found her slumped on the floor, gasping for breath. Jasmine's forehead was damp, but her body felt cold. She met his eyes, but hers were vacant. Bilal's breathing grew shallow, and sweat poured from his temples onto his bare chest, yet he mustered the courage to perform CPR on her. Jasmine's heart had stopped. Bilal screamed her name, a terrifying roar ripping from his chest.

He held her in his lap as he dialed for an ambulance, shaking so badly he almost dropped the phone. Jasmine was wearing a light muslin nightgown. In a panic, Bilal tore down the kitchen curtains, wrapped her in them, and lifted her into his arms.

By the time he reached the front door, the paramedics were already racing in with a stretcher. He pushed past them, shouting frantically for them to move aside as he carried her out. The hospital wasn't far from his house, but every second passed like an hour. Jasmine was unconscious. The nurses at the hospital tried to resuscitate her. But she was gone.

Bilal's mother said it must've been the evil eye that got her. She hated the idea of women sitting at weddings, staring at the bride and groom. "Their eyes can cut through rocks," she had said.

Abdullah tried numerous times to encourage Bilal to open up by sharing his own experience with depression after Ahmed was killed in the tunnel. But Bilal was stubborn.

Now, as Abdullah and Bilal settled in to talk, Habiba came in carrying a tray with two plates of cake. Abdullah watched her in amusement. She was like a tightrope walker, trying to keep her balance. "You need help with that, baby girl?" he offered, smiling.

"*Mashallah*. This beauty is yours?" Bilal teased, giving Habiba a warm nod. She set the tray down, put a plate in front of Bilal, and shook his hand. He kissed her hand. "*Shukran.*"

She walked over to Abdullah, placed the other plate in front of him, and whispered in his ear, "Baba, come and take the tea."

Abdullah stepped out and returned with a tray holding two cups. "I'll talk as you eat," he said.

"Or you could let me savor the taste for a minute." Bilal helped himself to a big chunk of the cake. He licked his lips. "Man, this cake is heaven. How does Um Omar do it? It's so moist."

Abdullah ignored the compliment. "*Sahtain.* I didn't ask you here to marvel at the cake. I got this suspicious text message from that woman, and I can't tell if it's real or utter *zift.*"

"Go ahead. I'm all ears," Bilal said.

Abdullah tossed the phone to him. Bilal read the message and went back to digging his fork into the cake. He was used to these kinds of stories. "This is the woman you have Salem tracking?"

"Yes."

"Tell me more about her."

"You know when you meet someone and feel a repellent force between you? She's like that. She tries to initiate conversations with me, and I always push her away… without being indecent."

"Is she attractive?"

Abdullah shot Bilal a cold glare. "What does that have to do with what we're talking about?" His voice rose a pitch too high, and he got up to shut the door.

"You're too serious, Abood. I'm just asking you to state the facts."

"Why don't you see her for yourself and decide?" Abdullah snorted.

"Is there anything suspicious about her?"

"She messages me a lot and keeps asking questions. Even my wife thinks she has an evil eye. And now she sends me this."

"She's infatuated. It's obvious," Bilal responded, gulping his tea.

Abdullah exhaled in frustration. "You're not being helpful. What do you make of this crappy message?!"

Bilal was unperturbed. He knew of agents who had tried to take down anyone, from ordinary citizens to Resistance fighters, and this seemed to fit the bill.

"Listen, Abood. If you intend to get to the bottom of this and find out what she's up to, you've got to respond." Abdullah grimaced at the idea as Bilal continued, "This woman could be one of two things. She's either just trying to get your attention and start a relationship, or she wants to lure you into something scandalous… maybe even for Israeli intelligence."

Abdullah's gaze drifted as he considered it, but he was satisfied with Bilal's answer. "See how you think after you eat," he quipped.

"So, you think the second scenario is more likely," Bilal observed. "In any case, it's all hypothetical. We need to investigate further to be sure. Tell her you'll help her out so you can see the man who allegedly harasses her."

Abdullah ran his hand through his hair as he leaned forward. "I don't want to give her the satisfaction of responding to her."

"Pride, my man. Or is it fear of Um Omar?" Bilal couldn't contain his mockery, but as he sat up, his tone turned serious. "Listen, habibi. You need to see this as a mission. This isn't just about you. This woman's message is blunt, to say the least. Telling you—a complete stranger—about sexual harassment! Would any girl in Gaza do that? Have you noticed anything odd lately while going about your days?"

Abdullah had been cautious with his movements and made sure to change his schedule often. "Why do you ask that?"

"Maybe someone leaked some info about you, and she's trying to drag you down that filthy pit first. You know the rest. She'd film it all... then blackmail you into working with her, and..."

"That's enough," Abdullah said, putting his hand up.

"Don't go anywhere alone until we sort this out. I'll assign two guys to shadow you. Adjust your schedule and stay armed whenever you go out," Bilal said, glancing at his watch. "I should be going. Thanks for the cake."

Ever since that old woman visited his mother, Abdullah had felt uneasy and tense. This wasn't helping at all. He didn't tell Fatina about his worries because it was the last thing she needed. For now, he had to respond to Dalia, even if it wasn't through a message. He'd appoint the right man for the job.

Chapter 14

Abdullah: Bilal's Life

Abdullah was never late—not even for gatherings with friends. Yet when he got to the beach, Bilal was already there. "*Salamat*. And I thought I was early," he said, sitting beside him on the concrete bench.

It was an hour before sunset. The benches lining the street offered visitors sweeping views of the two-toned water: a natural sea blue and a murky blue-green. Gaza's shoreline was contaminated by untreated sewage, a result of chronic electricity shortages.

Ever since Abdullah was little, he couldn't remember a single day of uninterrupted power. With every attack, the crisis worsened—fuel blockades and bombed power plants. Though man-made, it clung to life like a chronic disease with no cure in sight.

"Here," Abdullah handed Bilal a coffee. A medium-sized cup from a street stall was only two shekels. Bilal accepted it quietly.

This wasn't his usual jokester persona. When Abdullah had called Bilal earlier, saying he needed to discuss something important and suggesting the beach for their meeting, he suspected Bilal had realized it wouldn't be about work.

Abdullah cupped his coffee with both hands, letting its warmth travel up his arms. It was nearing the end of March, but the coolness of the air tingled across his skin.

"You can skip the small talk," Bilal started abruptly.

"You mean the philosophical blabber? I wasn't planning to preach."

"I'll put you at ease, Abood. I'm not thinking of remarrying," Bilal replied, tiredly, as if he had already said this a hundred times.

Abdullah studied his cup, silently urging Bilal to continue.

"Just so you can relax, the whole idea of marriage no longer interests me." Bilal gazed at the horizon. The golden-orange hues were fading, and the sun would soon sink.

Abdullah remembered how in love Bilal had been with Jasmine. "Bilal, you're capable of loving again, you just…"

"Abdullah, don't ever tell me to love! Love weakens the heart. I'm glad my work doesn't require emotion." Bilal's voice trembled with anger, his chest rising and falling heavily, but he continued. "She was born with a heart defect, I knew. During the Intifada, her mom inhaled tear gas while she was pregnant with her… I knew, but I didn't care."

He exhaled. "Remember, Abood, how you told me that when you meet the person you want to spend the rest of your life with, your heart speaks?"

"Absolutely."

Abdullah was instantly transported back to when he met Fatina.

He was filling in for a few hours at the stationery store his friend owned on Jalal Street, near a girls' high school. Fatina walked in with a friend. She initially chose a sketchbook and some drawing pencils. Then she added three tubes of acrylic paint. When she came to the counter to pay, she was twenty shekels short. Abdullah remembered how she pressed her lips together and rolled them inward. She dug into her bag and put all the money she had on the counter in front of him.

"This is all I have," she said, her cheeks glowing pink.

Abdullah tried to conceal his smile, but his emotions betrayed him. "You could wait until the owner comes back and see if he…"

Fatina's friend begged her, "You don't need these today. You could…"

"Yes, I do. For the horse portrait," Fatina shot back. Abdullah tried to busy himself with his phone as the two girls argued, ignoring his presence.

Fatina turned to him again. "The owner knows us. If you open that notebook, where he records all the debts, you'll see my name: Fatina." The friend side-eyed Fatina and nudged her foot, but she didn't budge.

Abdullah's gaze lingered on Fatina. There was a spark, and he found himself staring. She was determined to get those paints. He loved her spontaneity and passion. She was an artist. She'd made it easy for him to learn her name. Her name alone, which meant alluring, made his heart skip a beat. She consumed his thoughts, and he started inventing excuses to go to the stationery store, hoping to see her.

When he grew restless and uncertain about whether falling for a schoolgirl was right, he turned to Bilal.

"Are you telling me that you, Abdullah Mansour, are in love?" Bilal asked.

Abdullah felt exposed. "I knew you'd enjoy this," he said.

Bilal crossed his legs and moved his foot in circles. "Abood, the soldier. I imagine you're on night duty at the border, and instead of watching the enemy, you stargaze and see her face and…"

"I'm *ahbal* for coming to ask for your advice." Abdullah threw his hands up in the air.

Bilal sat up. "If this were back in March, and now we're halfway through June, she's no longer a schoolgirl. She should be getting ready for university." Then he leaned toward Abdullah, suddenly remembering something. "Our neighbor's daughter married at sixteen. I guess some girls don't mind."

Abdullah mulled it over for a moment. He could see himself standing in front of her. He recalled watching her hands as she fumbled for the money. Her fingers were slender, ideal for that artistic touch. He imagined her holding the pencil gracefully and drawing.

Bilal interrupted Abdullah's memories.

"Jasmine was the one. It's been two years, and when I think of her, I feel like she was never here. I ask myself: Were we married for real? Did I actually hold her? Make love to her? It's like a mirage." Bilal's voice was breaking. He bit his lip as if to keep his tears from spilling.

Abdullah felt a pang of sorrow. "Bilal, Jasmine is no longer part of this world. You have your own world to live in."

Bilal slumped back, drained of emotion. "Abdullah, all the love I had for her has turned to hate and revulsion! She's in Jannah now, and I'm in hell. She haunts my dreams, as if she's imprisoned my soul. She's gone… and she stole something from me." He clutched his chest before going on. "She's taken my heart. I've become numb to people, to things I used to enjoy, to everything! I'm her eternal prisoner. Sometimes I scream her name and plead with her to let me go, to free my soul!"

Bilal's cup fell to the ground. He hid his face in his hands, trembling all over. "*Wallah*, I hate her, I hate her…"

The emotional outpour sent shivers down Abdullah's spine. He squeezed Bilal's shoulder.

"You must think I'm sick and need help. But I tell you, no one can help me. She won't set me free," Bilal gasped between sobs.

Abdullah wasn't sure he had the psychological knowledge to help his friend, but he wasn't about to leave him a prisoner to his misery.

"You may never fall in love with another woman the way you did with Ja… with her, but you will find someone you feel at ease with. Your heart is in Allah's hands, and He can heal you. He can make you feel again."

"I don't miss her. I just want her to go away." Bilal's stare hardened.

Abdullah offered Bilal his coffee, which he drank quickly.

"Bilal, you've imprisoned your own soul. You've limited your vision to just one form of love. Look around you. There is so much to ponder. Just open your heart to everything that surrounds you in this world, and you'll start to feel again."

"How?"

"Think of your poor mother, for instance. She must be sick, seeing you like this. Take her out and talk to her. Don't shut yourself in like this. Don't let Jasmine imprison your soul. Discover yourself again. You talk to the school kids who buy candy from you, don't you? Think about what it would be like to have a child of your own."

Bilal watched the sun begin to dip. "The sun keeps rising every morning. It keeps rising," he echoed, as if testing the truth of it.

This sudden revival gave Abdullah some hope. "See, habibi, your wisdom is ineffable. You've got to rise again. Don't let anything beat you. You've said it so wonderfully yourself."

"Don't tell my mother a word of this, or she'll be out searching for a bride. You know how she is. She used to give me lists of potential brides, but when she noticed I ignored her attempts, she stopped. I feel bad for her. I wasn't nice…" Bilal said sadly.

Abdullah was grateful that Bilal had vented and released some of the built-up pressure.

"Listen, why don't you start with her?" he suggested. "Let's go buy her a present, something to lift her spirits."

Bilal nodded. "My mother has tolerated my shitty behavior the most. I owe her a lot. And maybe you can come with me. She'd love to see you."

Chapter 15

Abdullah: Suspicion

"Abood, that woman at the club…" began Fatina.

"Yeah, the one in red?"

"She gave me the creeps with her stares. I trust my intuition." She crossed her arms. "She's got an evil eye, is what I think. You may laugh, but I just feel it."

Abdullah didn't undermine his wife's instincts. He was just as uneasy about Dalia's presence, but his fears were of a different kind. What if she were an agent? Abdullah wasn't paranoid, but living in Gaza and being in the Resistance demanded constant vigilance.

"You know, Abood, I think she's trying to get your… to get men's attention at the club. I don't believe she's a writer," Fatina said, unabashed.

Abdullah knew Fatina would have a fit if she found out what kind of messages Dalia had sent him. Luckily, he had a habit of changing his number from time to time.

"You don't need to worry about her too much. She did write something, and she's scheduled to read it soon."

Fatina clenched her teeth, then exhaled, and began twirling a strand of hair—a habit she'd never shaken. Abdullah guided Fatina's hand away from her hair and drew an arm around her waist. "You've become an expert on human behavior. Do you imagine that all writers write about love, peace, and justice? I hate to disappoint you, but many write trash."

"If I were a writer, I'd write about… I'd write about you," Fatina said, slipping her arms around Abdullah's neck. "About how your jade-green eyes match your military uniform, how you still have a soft face and a…"

"You could draw me," Abdullah coaxed her. "Remember, you once promised me… years ago."

The moment Abdullah mentioned the subject again, Fatina blinked back tears. He held her close and whispered, "I fell in love with your art, remember? How about we go to the craft shop and…" Fatina lowered her eyes, staying silent. Abdullah kissed her fingertips. "You can still paint. Don't let your talent go to waste."

He knew it was a sensitive topic. It had been years since her hand was permanently damaged, and she still wrapped it when she went out so people wouldn't see it. Abdullah repeatedly reassured her that her good hand was fine and that she could still paint, that he loved her no matter what, and that she needed to remember all the other blessings she had. But it was the same every time. She'd simply say, "It's about how I feel inside."

***

Abdullah and Bilal consulted their engineer about installing a surveillance camera on the seventh floor. But when Salem reported that the woman had entered an apartment on the sixth floor, they had to change their plans.

"We need to find a way to get into the apartment," Bilal said. "We'll have someone cut off the water supply to the sixth, seventh, and eighth floors. Then Nafez will go in as a plumber."

The following day, Abdullah and Salem waited at one of their offices while Bilal and Nafez carried out the operation. After they returned, Nafez recounted the events.

At the Al-Safa building, they needed to distract the caretaker—not that he ever paid much attention. Bilal could hear the clink of coins from the man's phone, the unmistakable sound of the game Subway Surfers. Nafez took the elevator to the sixth floor.

"Remember what you're going to say," Bilal whispered before the elevator door shut. "I'll be nearby in case anything happens."

Nafez nodded.

He got to apartment 608 and pressed the doorbell. It rang three times before the door slowly opened. A middle-aged man with disheveled hair and a scrawny face carefully kept the door from opening wide. He sized up Nafez, tense with irritation at being disturbed.

"Asalamu alaikum," Nafez said, as if he were reciting a recorded message. "We're doing maintenance on the water system, and I'm inspecting the apartments."

The man assessed him, his features taut. "Yeah, but I didn't call anybody."

"Well, some residents complained about water issues, so I'm inspecting the pipes."

"So, you have to do this from the inside?"

It was clear the guy wasn't going to let him in, but Nafez had already captured everything he needed with the hidden camera on his cap.

"How about I go around to the other apartments and come back?" Nafez suggested.

"If the problem persists, you can come back in an hour."

After inspecting a few apartments, Nafez returned to 608. He rang the bell three times. No answer.

Back at the office, Nafez uninstalled the camera and connected it to the laptop. "Here's our guy," he said as Abdullah came over to stand behind him. Salem followed, crossing his arms. "Anyone recognize him?"

Salem stared at the screen and muttered something Abdullah couldn't quite hear. Before he could ask, Bilal came in carrying a coffee pot and some paper cups.

"Let me see," he said, setting the coffee on the table and turning the laptop toward himself. His eyebrows shot up in astonishment as he zoomed in on the man's face.

"What? You've seen him?" Abdullah asked, his pulse quickening.

Bilal turned to Abdullah, eyes wide. "Abdullah, this man is your new neighbor."

Chapter 16

Salem: A Task

"Listen to me, Salem. That girl, Dalia..." Abdullah said as they sat in Salem's office.

"Abdullah, I've still been following her. After the last writers' club meeting, she came out of the sixth-floor apartment around 9:30 with that other woman again. They were dressed in totally different clothing and had their faces covered. They got into a car, and I pursued them. Dalia had dinner with the driver. I saw her face while she was eating."

"Awesome. We need to find out the exact connection between her and the man Bilal identified as my new neighbor, Masood," Abdullah said. "I already have my suspicions about his whole family. We have to know what Dalia is leading me to. I know you won't like the sound of this, but I need you to give this girl some attention at the next club meeting so she confides in you."

Salem got up, walked to the window, and pushed it open. He'd been working undercover for four years and had successfully completed all his missions. But this was a first of its kind. "What do you mean, give her attention? You know I can't..."

Abdullah told Salem about the message and how he could very well be a target for someone bigger than Dalia, trying in vain to ease the tension surrounding the mission. "You'd just spend time chatting with her at the club and text her a lot when you get home. You'll have to be charming…"

Salem had his hands in his pockets. "You expect me to flirt with her?"

"Habibi, I'm not asking you to go on a date with her—just talking and texting," Abdullah retorted. "It's a duty, and I can't find a better expert than you for it. Once we have enough information, I'll pull you out."

Salem thought it over. He didn't know how he'd approach the matter, but he was already attending the club meetings undercover.

"What if she's not interested?"

"Text her day and night. Say good morning, afternoon, evening, sweet dreams. Pretend to share some personal stuff about yourself. And remember to get a new phone number for this mission."

Salem walked home that evening, drowning in thought and grappling with the task ahead. He'd always shouldered his responsibilities with passion and precision. Disguising himself as a college student was enough for him. Now he had to charm some woman who might, in all likelihood, turn out to be a spy for the enemy.

Putting personal feelings aside, what Abdullah said troubled Salem. What if she was after Abdullah? Salem knew that Israeli intelligence was constantly recruiting Palestinians as spies through blackmail. He needed to perform this duty with extreme caution.

When he got home, Salem found nine messages on his phone. They were all from his fiancée, Yumna. "Damn! My idiot brain forgot," he said to himself in disbelief.

Salem, you said you were coming over. I waited. I'm still waiting. Yumna had sent the last message over an hour ago.

Abdullah's mission had consumed his thoughts. It was 9:00 now. For Yumna's family, it might as well have been midnight. He decided to call her anyway. Yumna picked up on the fourth ring.

"Hello."

"Hey, baby. Did I wake you up?"

"*Marhaba...*"

"I'm sorry. I had an unexpected appointment," he said. Yumna was silent for a moment before Salem heard her sobs. "Hey, what's wrong?"

"Nothing...I don't want to talk right now."

"I'm coming over. I don't care if it's late."

"No, please don't. You know how Baba feels about late-night visits. I'll be fine. I just had a stressful day, and I wanted to see you."

"How about we have breakfast tomorrow morning?" Salem suggested. "I'll bring *manakeesh.*"

Yumna's sobbing quieted. He could hear her sniffle and try to clear her throat. "Okay. I love you," she eventually said.

Salem was highly intuitive and intelligent—qualities that made him well-suited to an undercover role. But the inconsistency of his work schedule was agonizing. He needed to sort this out before the wedding to prevent problems in his marriage.

Yumna was a lovely girl of natural, unembellished beauty who captivated him. They'd been engaged for three months now. She wanted to settle down. Her living circumstances had become unbearable since her mother was killed a year ago.

Yumna's family was sleeping when an Israeli airstrike hit their downstairs neighbor's home, killing a Resistance fighter and his family. Yumna's floor shook, and all the windows shattered. Her parents' bedroom wall collapsed onto her mother. She was pulled from under the debris—dead.

Aside from the trauma, Yumna had to take on all the household responsibilities, including caring for her ten- and twelve-year-old brothers. Salem suggested that her dad needed to remarry, but she didn't take it well.

Chapter 17

Abdullah: The March

"We're all set, kids. Let's go," Abdullah called out as he carried a canvas bag filled with food and water.

It was March 30, and the Great March of Return was about to take place. After a few meetings, the organizing committee agreed that families across the Gaza Strip should mobilize together. The committee had stationed buses at various pickup points. Abdullah was taking his family in their own car.

When he walked into his mom's apartment, Um Abdullah was overjoyed. This would be her first glimpse of her homeland since 1967. She had woken up early, baked some pastries, and packed them in plastic containers. He instantly recognized the aroma of thyme-filled pastries.

Um Abdullah grinned broadly as she put the containers into a bag. "You want a za'atar? Your favorite."

It took a lot of force for her to open the container. Her gold bracelets jingled. Abdullah wondered how she never took them off. He'd seen her wearing them all her life. They were part of her gold dowry, and she cherished them. She gave her son a pastry.

Um Abdullah wore her Palestinian dress—black with vibrant red, green, and white stitching. She often boasted of having embroidered it herself. A white cotton hijab was draped loosely over her head, and she carried the Palestinian flag. Her face brightened with a smile, and a quiet joy shimmered across it.

Abdullah's heart warmed at the sight of his mother. He hadn't seen her this happy in a long time. She looked as if she were returning to her homeland for real.

"Abdullah, my legs are in perfect shape today. I don't feel any pain in my knees."

Abdullah hugged his mother and planted a kiss on her forehead. "You're the most beautiful Falastiniyya ever," he said.

Um Abdullah moved with an unsteady gait, swaying from side to side to show her son she was in good shape. But this didn't stop Abdullah from holding her hand as they left the house.

Twenty minutes later, they reached the encampment area near the separation fence. Traffic was at a standstill. Buses, cars, and donkey and horse carts all mingled as if in a chaotic parade. There was an incredible thrill in the air. Abdullah hoped it would be safe and that the day would end peacefully.

His mind was crammed with history. Seventy years of displacement and dispossession. Like many Palestinians displaced before him in 1948, Abdullah's father fled to the Gaza Strip in 1967, just one year after he and Abdullah's mother had married. Yet hope, even if it flickered at times, was the shining light that never fully faded from Abdullah's heart. The Great March of Return would be a critical chapter in the history of the Palestinian struggle for freedom and justice.

"Baba, are we going to Siddo's house in our other country?" Omar asked, leaning forward from the back seat to catch his father's attention.

Abdullah tried to think of an answer Omar could digest, but all he could come up with was, "We'll see when we get there."

Fatina had tried to explain to their kids, in the simplest way possible, what the March was about. However, in their young minds, nothing made sense unless they saw it for themselves.

"We're going to see our land from afar, habibi," Um Abdullah responded. "And I'm going to let you hold the flag."

When they reached the camp, they still had to walk about ten minutes—the roads were crowded with parked vehicles. Rows of tents had been set up, each bearing the name of a Palestinian city: Haifa, Yaffa, Al-Quds, Akka, Al-Khalil…

It was a warm spring day, and the sun was a welcome sight after a cold winter. Winters in Gaza weren't long, but there was a chilly period that typically lasted some forty days. Abdullah raised his head to soak up the warmth. The sun tickled his face.

When they finally reached the encampment, Fatina spread a blanket on the ground, but no one sat down.

"Abdullah, show me the land now." Um Abdullah reached for her son's arm, her expression full of childlike awe. "If I sit, it'll be hard for me to get back up."

The area where Abdullah's family stood was elevated and about 700 meters from the separation fence. Abdullah gazed east. From his position, he had a bird's-eye view of the whole scene. The protestors kept their attention fixed in the same direction, toward the lands on the other side of the fence. Beyond the waves of people, vast green spaces stretched out on the other side.

They were caged in a big prison, with their oppressors positioned along the frontier on small dunes. Snipers lay there with their high-tech weapons. Everyone and everything was within their range.

Although the view didn't offer much, the expansive landscape instantly affected Um Abdullah. Her voice trembled as she took it all in.

"Your father always believed he would return. Repeatedly, he insisted it was only a matter of time. But he's gone, and here I am. One day, I'll be gone too. If only I could go back, see my house, and smell the soil of my garden, I'd be content to die there, on my land."

Abdullah felt his throat tighten. He had heard those words before, so many times.

This was a hard moment for everyone. An onslaught of thoughts overwhelmed Abdullah. Why couldn't they return to their land? Why had they been forced to live, generation after generation, in camps receiving relief aid when they had their own land they could go back to and cultivate?

Abdullah put his arms around his mother and lightly rubbed her shoulder. He breathed deeply and steadied himself, always trying to be the strong one. "Come on, Yumma. You were cheerful on your way here. What's all this gloomy talk? Insha'Allah, we'll return. Now, come on, raise your flag high and let's take some pictures."

Fatina stood nearby with Habiba and Omar beside her. Pointing towards the fence, she was trying to explain where they were and what they were seeing on the other side. It was Fatina's first visit to this area, and she looked overwhelmed with a mix of excitement, nostalgia, and hopelessness. She choked on her words as she pointed to the land. Abdullah could see her fighting back tears. "See those vast green areas? That's our land."

"I don't see Siddo's house," said Omar, his eyes flicking left and right.

Abdullah walked over and lifted Omar onto his shoulders. "Can you see farther now? Tell me what you see."

He felt a tangible sense of imprisonment. All the people he saw, along with the rest of the two million population, were being held captive on a piece of land that was constantly under attack. He placed his arm around

Fatina's shoulder, again trying to steady himself. She leaned into him as silent tears tumbled down her cheeks.

"The weather is amazing, isn't it?" Abdullah offered, hoping to cheer her up, but what he really wanted was a good, long cry.

Haunting memories gripped him. He remembered his martyred comrades, his long nights in the Resistance tunnels, the ongoing Israeli attacks, the night Fatina was seriously wounded and her left hand maimed for life, and the trauma she suffered and its lingering effects, which resurfaced at random.

The shouts and joyful shrieks of children playing brought him back to the March.

Multiple generations surrounded him: grandparents, mothers, fathers, and kids. Many women were embroidering pieces. A larger group gathered around a wide cloth, stitching a map of Palestine. On a central stage, dabke dancers warmed up for a performance. People danced, ate, delivered impassioned speeches, raised banners, and walked towards the fence to get a closer look. A bystander might think they were celebrating the actual return to their homeland—unaware of what lay ahead.

The snipers were in position, but the young Palestinian men were fearless. A group got close to the fence. Gunshots shattered the peace and joy. The occupying soldiers opened fire. People sprinted back to the camp areas. Ambulance sirens pierced the air.

One man was shot dead. He'd be dubbed the first martyr of the Great March of Return.

***

The following week, families marched again.

Young men grew creative in confronting the snipers. Resistance music blared from loudspeakers as the *kawshook* unit's truck trundled down the bumpy dirt road. The men swiftly unloaded the tires, passing them to one another before setting them ablaze. Thick black smoke rose and blew east toward the snipers, blocking their line of sight. The men kept feeding the fire with rubber. Their faces and arms were blackened with soot.

Abdullah contemplated their fearlessness and bravery. Most of them were teenagers and twenty-somethings who'd spent their entire lives under war and siege. It was all they knew. This was a generation with nothing to look forward to and nothing to lose.

Israeli snipers attacked the protesters with tear gas and live bullets. More people were killed and injured. Many were permanently maimed. Dozens became amputees. They'd eventually witness journalists shot in the eye and paramedics killed while trying to rescue injured protesters. The medical personnel believed their MEDIC-marked neon vests offered them protection and safety. They were wrong. No one was safe.

Abdullah's family sat atop a small dune about three hundred meters from the fence. They could see the snipers on the hills and hiding behind metal barricades. Abdullah knew the snipers had an equally clear view—every movement, every detail exposed—making everyone an easy target.

"My stomach is in knots," Fatina said, her eyes finding Abdullah's. "I'm energized to come to the March and take part in a historic event with the people. But, look, Abood. We're not safe like peaceful protestors should be. Why is everything different when it comes to us? Why are we always seen as lesser humans?!"

For once, Abdullah couldn't find the words to comfort her. Now, it was the third week of protest, close to 5:00 p.m., and many protesters began walking toward the buses. Fatina got up and called for the kids to come. Abdullah was holding his mother's hand. As they started climbing the dune, the piercing sound of bullets made them all involuntarily duck. It all happened too quickly to comprehend.

Screams echoed through the air.

Voices shouted, "The boy! Get an ambulance here!"

Abdullah let go of his mother's hand and ran in the opposite direction.

"Omar!"

He turned back to see Fatina, paralyzed with fear. She couldn't get up, but her eyes followed their son as he lay on a stretcher. Abdullah pushed the stretcher into the ambulance.

Chapter 18

Fatina: The Hospital

Two ROWS of connected metal chairs lined the corridor outside the operating room at Nasser Hospital. The squeaking of cheap clogs would have been irritating, but Fatina's brain was blank. She curled up on the floor against the steel frame of a chair, clutching it for support. It was ice-cold. She couldn't tell whether she was shivering from the cold or from the fear surging through her.

Her son was still in the operating room. She struggled to understand what had happened, but it all felt so distant now. The clamor, the running, the shooting, the screams. She was trapped in the heavy silence of that moment.

Blurred images flickered at the edge of her vision. Sickly green uniforms and the robotic movement of a huge mop. She only saw the fibers, filthy gray, like unwashed hair. Was someone holding it, or did it move back and forth on its own?

As the door swung open, her stomach dropped, expecting the worst. Where was Abdullah? She only remembered sitting beside him in the ambulance as they were rushed away after the gunshots.

"Abdullah!" she called out, her voice hoarse.

She needed to try harder, but a pained screech escaped her mouth instead, echoing through the corridor. The white walls closed in around her like a death shroud. The mopping stopped.

"Where is your dad, young lady?" the janitor asked indifferently.

Did she really look like a child crouched there?

From the far end of the hall, a figure ran towards her. She couldn't quite make out who it was. As he got closer, she heard him calling her name. A sharp, trembling dread gripped her chest as she recognized the voice. She jolted to her feet as if struck by an electric shock, then froze.

It was her brother, Hamza.

Just seeing him reenergized her soul. But all she could do was wail in his arms. Suddenly, Fatina pulled away. She searched Hamza's face for answers.

"Where's Abdullah? Is Omar alive?! Hamza, answer me!"

Hamza held his sister's arms and sat her down. He opened a bottle of water and lifted it to her lips, as if it could extinguish the fire in her heart. Fatina felt a cold gush circulate through her body. She hadn't consumed anything in hours.

Wiping Fatina's tears with a tissue, Hamza gently tucked a loose strand of hair back beneath her hijab as he seemed to gather his nerves to deliver bad news.

"Omar is fine. He's alive. You hear me?"

Hamza repeated it a few times until relief flickered across Fatina's face.

"Then what…what are they doing to him now?"

"Fatina, your son is alive. But Omar's leg was badly hurt."

She tried to focus on her brother, but her vision blurred, and his face seemed distant. Slowly, she released her grip and slumped in the chair.

Images of amputees flashed before her: three young men arriving at the March on crutches. Each had lost a leg, yet they had returned to the protest.

Now her son would be one of them.

Chapter 19

Yumna: Opening Up

THE MORNING AFTER Salem missed Yumna's calls, he arrived at her home at 9:00 a.m. sharp. She opened the door and greeted him with a long, warm hug. "I missed you," she murmured against his chest.

After they shared breakfast, Salem placed his hand over Yumna's and rubbed it thoughtfully. "You may think this is insensitive, but I need to tell you something," he began, taking a deep breath. "Your dad needs someone to take care of him and your brothers."

She swallowed hard, tears slipping free despite herself. It was something she expected to hear again, but also feared. "I worry about my little brothers. They keep asking me if I'm going to live with them after we get married. I can't imagine someone in my mom's room and… things."

Salem moved closer and held her tightly, the lavender scent of her hair filling his nostrils. "We'll find the right person for your dad. You know he's like your brothers. He needs someone to keep him company and care for him. Imagine his loneliness. I'm sure he keeps up a brave front for your and your brothers' sake."

Yumna didn't think of it that way. She assumed that, with her mother gone, her father wouldn't be interested in companionship.

Salem tried to reassure her. "I know you're wondering how he could ever love again. Believe me, your mom will always be his only love, but he needs someone."

Ever since they got engaged, Yumna had avoided talking about her mother's killing, and Salem hadn't pushed her. He gave her a gentle, reassuring squeeze. "There's something in your eyes, Yumna."

She looked up at him. "What do you mean?"

Salem cupped her face. "There are words, so many of them, screaming to be said. I know this is painful, but you still haven't told me about that night. I can hold space for you to share."

Yumna let go of Salem and pushed herself back on the sofa for support. "Oh, Salem, it's too horrible to speak of."

Her expression went blank, but she continued.

"We were all asleep that night. It was nearly 2 a.m. I didn't hear the explosions. I was awakened by rubble hitting me. I dug my way out and ran to my brothers' room. They were screaming. I hugged them and called out for Baba, then I ran to my mom's room. She was alone. The blast force of the airstrike tore through our wall, bringing it down in a crash that buried everything in the room, including Mama. Baba and I dug her out from under the rubble. Blood gushed out of her mouth, and she was taking her last breath…"

Yumna's breathing hitched as she spoke. A tight, overwhelming pressure rose in her chest, as if everything inside her were about to break loose. She pressed her palm to her chest, crying and gasping for air.

"I never thought I'd live to see her die… like that. She was supposed to be at my wedding and hold her grandchildren…"

Holding her protectively, Salem placed his hand on Yumna's head and recited verses from the Quran. He offered her water and waited until her breathing eased. "I'm sorry, habibti," he whispered.

"Salem, I can never get over it, never forget it," she said.

"No one could ever forget something like that," Salem replied empathetically. "But life has a way of moving along, and leaves us no choice but to somehow move with it. I'm so sorry if this sounds insensitive, but that's how it is, isn't it?"

Yumna let out a muffled "yes."

After the Israeli warplanes attacked that night, a spokesperson for the occupying military announced that the target was an Islamic Jihad commander who lived on the floor below Yumna's home. The airstrike killed the commander, his wife, and two of their children. Two others survived.

"I keep thinking about those two kids and how they lost both their parents. It's so cruel," Yumna said.

"I agree, but I like to believe Allah will send compassionate people to take care of them. With time, you'll also get better. I promise. We'll also help your dad move forward, okay?" Salem lovingly stroked Yumna's long brown hair, playing with a few strands. "And we'll be there for your brothers, too."

Yumna's tension eased. His words reassured her. "I'll talk to my aunt. She always brings it up anyway," she said.

Salem's face lit up. He gently tilted her chin up and asked, "Does this mean we can set our wedding date?"

Yumna's smile came easily. "Baba's first."

Chapter 20

Dalia: A Message

DALIA WAS SLEEPLESS. Masood's threats were serious, and she couldn't see a way out. Their constant moving from house to house meant they had no relationships with neighbors or anyone at all. This kind of life alienated her from humanity.

She felt disgrace, humiliation, and utter disgust at what had become of her. Thoughts of her ex-husband filled Dalia with contempt. But was it really his fault, or had she too easily succumbed to Masood's domineering nature and threats?

Dalia texted Salem. *Hi, it's Dalia. I really need a favor from you. Can you help?*

It was after midnight. She would go to sleep if she could, keeping the phone close in case Salem answered. Lately, she had been suffering from insomnia. It was the constant overthinking and stress.

Her phone blinked with his reply. *Sure. What can I do for you?*

I need to speak with Abdullah, she typed back. *I saw you talking to him at the writers' club. Are you guys close? Could you ask him if he'd be willing to talk? A friend is in trouble, and she said he can help. It's serious.*

Another quick response. *I'm not on personal terms with the guy, but I can try to approach him as a colleague at the writers' club.*

She thought about the way Salem approached her at the club. It was strange how he suddenly became interested in her. Judging by his behavior and appearance, he seemed like a teenager. She grimaced, thinking of those types of men—the ones who flirted with girls just for the sake of it. If Salem had been her target, her job would've been much easier.

She clenched her teeth, disgusted with herself for how instinctively her mind reached for the methods she had been trained to use to manipulate men.

But she had been assigned to Abdullah Mansour. He was the first target who hadn't expressed interest in her. He lowered his gaze while talking to her, which made her feel low. He'd never shown even the faintest hint of indecency. She had to admit he was ethical… with a personality and good looks. His composed presence was quietly commanding yet free of the filth and menace that always seemed to cling to Masood.

Chapter 21

Abdullah: The Sea

Only early mornings were serene in Abdullah's city. So he always made sure to stay up after Fajr prayer to take advantage of those precious minutes of stillness.

He drew in the salty sea air. A jog along the beach was the remedy for all his anxieties. It reminded him that some things in life remained within his control. No one could take these moments from him.

Close to 6 o'clock, some early walkers would start to trickle in. But right now, he heard only nature—the cries of seagulls and the crescendo of the waves. Not far from shore, fishing boats dotted the sea. Nine nautical miles was the furthest they were permitted to go. Even within that limit, Israeli naval vessels sometimes opened fire on them. Faces of fishermen who had been killed flashed before Abdullah, but he pushed the images aside.

This moment was his.

April mornings still carried that biting chill. He started jogging slowly, then gradually increased his pace. As he picked up speed, warmth spread through Abdullah's body. He ran for ten-minute intervals. Energy surged through his legs. His lungs filled with the fresh morning breeze. It was the purest air, invigorating him. His mind was liberated. Weakness and negative energy dissipated with every step.

Abdullah reflected on how free he was despite the occupation. Free because others were imprisoned in Israeli prisons. Free because some couldn't run or even walk. That's when reality hit him. Freedom was a fragile word. He thought of his son.

Doctors had no choice but to amputate Omar's leg. The bullet had pulverized the tissue, bones, and arteries, making it impossible to save it. Abdullah had been with Omar at the hospital. He'd sought a counselor because, for the first time in his life, he felt helpless and couldn't find a way to cope with his son's loss.

As these thoughts invaded, he ran faster. The thudding of his feet pounded in his ears. He sprinted past a lush area of green grape vines, the rebuilt mosque after the last attack, and the greenhouses that, from a distance, looked like eggshells. There was no one around.

He made an abrupt right turn toward a raised area, ran down a hill, and when he reached the sandy beach, a choked cry escaped him, mixing with the roar of the waves. Pulling off his shirt and running shoes, Abdullah waded into the waves. The freezing water hit him hard. He gasped at first, then let it wash over him.

Lifting his arms, he began swimming. Within a few seconds, he was numb from the cold. The intensity of the waves and the cold washed away all his thoughts. He needed this badly. The sea was overpowering. He could almost hear it speaking to him as he merged with the waves.

He strained to hear what the sea was trying to tell him. Then he heard it: "The blows of life are what make you stronger." The sea was his ally. There was harmony between them. Just as the waves are relentless, he must resolve to be an ocean of strength.

When Abdullah got home, Fatina was still asleep. He walked in, his sweatpants dripping water onto the floor. Habiba was lying on the couch. She watched the puddle forming at Abdullah's feet. "I'll wipe this up before Mama wakes up. Don't worry," Abdullah said before heading to the bathroom.

After he changed and came back out into the living room, Habiba was on her phone. He sat beside her, kissed her forehead, and peeked at the screen. "You're up early."

"I had a dream that Omar could walk again. I was holding his hand at first, but then he walked all by himself."

Abdullah still felt mentally sharp after the jog and swim. He put his arm around his daughter. "So, what are you searching for on your phone, baby?"

"I searched for how to make someone who lost his leg walk again. I got some results."

The caring nature and innocence of his nine-year-old tugged at Abdullah's soul. Habiba pointed her phone at Abdullah. "It says he can have a plastic leg. He can even play football. Omar will like this, Baba," she said.

Abdullah had already visited the hospital to learn about the procedure for a prosthetic. Omar would need some therapy sessions beforehand. Thinking of all the physical and emotional turmoil they collectively endured, Abdullah wondered if all his people needed therapy. Hardly anyone spoke of receiving treatment, whether after an attack or from the ongoing toll of being shackled under the suffocating siege imposed on their land. People just went back to life and kept enduring.

Chapter 22

Abdullah: Confession

ABDULLAH RECEIVED A CALL from Salem, asking him to come to his office. When he arrived, Bilal was also there. Salem showed them the messages from Dalia.

Bilal insisted, "Abdullah, you have no choice. You're talking to this woman. I'll take precautions and have men stationed outside the building."

Abdullah was growing restless with the whole situation. He wanted to get to the bottom of it quickly. "Okay, I'll do it," he replied instantly.

"That's my man." Bilal slapped him on the shoulder.

Before leaving, Abdullah turned to Salem. "Hey, can I have a minute?"

Salem was distracted. He stood, but Abdullah motioned for him to sit. "I'm sorry I never got to thank you for your awesome work. I know it came at a crucial time in your personal life."

"It's all right," Salem said, sitting with his hands folded. "I'm hoping to get married in two months. We just need to settle a few matters."

Throughout his life in the Resistance, Abdullah had come to understand the true meaning of camaraderie. He constantly reminded himself to care for his comrades. Salem had once told him about Yumna's mother and how Yumna was still traumatized.

"Listen, Um Omar wants to visit Yumna. She's been wanting to for some time, but with Omar, it hasn't been easy."

"That'd be really nice. *Shukran*," Salem said.

***

Abdullah arrived at the library to meet Dalia at the designated time. He didn't know what to expect. When he entered, Dalia was perched on the edge of her seat, fidgeting and biting her lip. She wore a black hijab and no makeup. Her eyebrows were furrowed, and her face was pale and stony. She didn't get up to greet him. Abdullah pulled out a chair and sat down.

"I really appreciate your willingness to help," she said. "I know you may have reason to doubt what I'm about to tell you, but please trust me. If you don't want to help, I understand."

She exhaled through pursed lips.

"I have a friend who is involved in something bad, and she needs help. She can't extricate herself from the group she's working with. Where should she go? They've threatened her life." Dalia's voice cracked as she finished.

Abdullah noticed tears forming. She didn't try to hide them. Her hands trembled as she sat there. "Could you be more specific?" he asked.

"She's involved in espionage," Dalia said plainly.

Abdullah looked to the floor for a moment before meeting Dalia's eyes. "These kinds of cases go to Palestinian intelligence."

"If she wanted to confess, be interrogated, and be imprisoned for Allah knows how long, she would've done that," Dalia stated coldly. "But she…she asked me to see if there was someone who could help. Her own brother is threatening her, so it's hard for her to escape."

Abdullah understood that Dalia was making her confession right then and there.

"I'm not authorized to act on behalf of intelligence," he replied carefully. "I could get in trouble if I tried to help her. I can only offer her some friendly advice."

"Please do." Dalia pressed on, her words rushing together. "This friend is in a very vulnerable state. I have to assure her she's safe, or she may…take her own life. She has kids, and she's their only provider. If she can't be assured, this conversation can end right now."

It was clear that Dalia needed to make it known how she wanted things to play out. Abdullah saw both determination and sadness on her face, and he could feel the mix of contempt, remorse, and vehemence in her tone.

She turned away, dabbed at her lashes, then faced Abdullah again. "I'll be honest with you. I know you're a righteous and virtuous person, and I'm sorry for offending you with my initial inappropriateness. But I want you to know that wasn't the real me."

She wept softly. Her sentences tangled with sobs as she tried to steady herself amid the chaos of words erupting after what Abdullah imagined were months of suppression. "I have an old mother, two kids to care for, and no one to turn to. If I turn myself in, will they prosecute me or give me a chance to redeem myself?"

Abdullah sat, unblinking. His jaw was stiff from clenching his teeth. He tried to grasp the enormity of what he had just heard while weighing his response.

"I think it depends on whether you've been involved in putting people's lives at risk. Either way, you'd still be jailed until your case is resolved. For your safety and to make sure your brother doesn't harm you, I can have someone pass his details to intelligence. In the meantime, to avoid raising suspicion, tell him you're getting closer to your current target."

Dalia looked into Abdullah's face, obviously evaluating the proposal, then said, "I'll give you the details now."

She wrote her brother's name and one of the phone numbers she used when calling him on a piece of paper and handed it to Abdullah. He again instructed Dalia to tell Masood that she was making real progress and that it would only be a matter of days before her target gave something up.

Chapter 23

Fatina: Fury

It was nearly 7 p.m. when Fatina finally put the kids to sleep and headed into the kitchen to make something to eat. It had been a long day. Omar was in one of his moods, a habit he had developed since his amputation. He had refused to go to school today. Fatina tried to coax him. "You know your friends will miss you. They're playing football after school, and Baba said you could go with them," she said.

All her days had become a tug-of-war of coaxing, uplifting, and soothing, which drained her energy. Sometimes, Omar would listen to Habiba more than to Fatina—and even more to Abdullah.

One day, she had broken down and told Abdullah she needed a break. He walked in and found her stuffing clothes into a tote bag.

"Hey," Abdullah began gingerly.

"Abood, I'm going to spend a day or two at my parents' place," she said, trying to stay composed. She moved to the dresser, grabbed her deodorant and brush, and tossed them into the bag.

It was unlike Fatina to spend nights alone at her parents' place. Whenever she went, the kids would always be with her. She thought it through, but no option felt fair. She wasn't trying to rebel against anyone. She just needed a break.

Abdullah snatched the bag from her, threw it behind him, and pulled Fatina into his arms.

"Please, Abood! Just let me go," Fatina pleaded, barely able to speak.

He sighed and said in a hoarse voice, "You need a break from me, too?"

Fatina felt a pang of guilt. It was true she had to manage Omar's challenges and moods, but she knew Abdullah was trying to support her. He had started taking days off, coming home earlier, and taking them out.

"No. Omar's just been giving me a hard time," she sobbed into Abdullah's shirt.

He gently rested his hand on her back, stroking in slow circles. "We both need a break. How about we go away for a day or two, and the kids can stay with your parents?"

Fatina's crying subsided. "We can do that?"

"Go pack a bigger bag," Abdullah said.

They had spent two nights at a chalet owned by one of Abdullah's friends. It was a small place, tucked away in a garden with a swimming pool.

She couldn't remember the last time she and Abdullah had shared a freely intimate moment since their first child was born. As they talked for hours, she felt how long it had been since they'd had a real conversation—the kind not interrupted by children calling or quarrelling.

Sitting under the stars, Fatina asked Abdullah about the constellations. He was the one who had taught her how to stargaze. Fatina felt her breathing ease as she marveled at the sky. There was a Creator behind it all. The sense of peace helped her think clearly. She found herself saying, "Abood, Allah takes care of the whole universe. He'll take care of us."

The quiet moments together had given her more hope.

With their little getaway drifting through her thoughts, Fatina decided to make a quick salad and toast with *labneh*. She laid out all the vegetables on the counter and had just started dicing the tomatoes when Abdullah's phone beeped. A message. It lit up the screen, glaring at her.

> *I wanted to thank you for helping me. If it weren't*
> *for you...*

Fatina froze—the knife in one hand, the phone in the other. She opened the full message.

> *my life would've been destroyed. I owe you so*
> *much.*
> *I thought a lot before writing this. I know it's*
> *risky. But what is life without risks?*
> *I know I don't deserve this, but please give me a*
> *chance to be part of your world.*

Fatina's eyes darted across the screen as she tried to make sense of the message. Unwelcome, wild stories flooded her mind.

> *I don't think there's any man out there who is like*
> *you in empathy, kindness, and courage. I've never*
> *felt loved in my life. It's been years of abuse and*
> *torture for me. Your kindness has touched a deep*
> *place in my heart.*
> *D*

Fatina remembered a neighbor whose husband had taken a second wife, one of his co-workers. She thought about how spending at least seven hours a day with someone at work often meant they saw each other more than they saw their own spouses. But Abdullah's work didn't involve women. The writers' club was the only setting where he interacted with them.

Still holding the knife she had been using to dice the tomatoes, Fatina screamed as the blade slipped and cut her finger. She reached for the paper towels, but the roll unraveled and tumbled to the floor. She tore off a handful and wrapped the wound. It was deeper than she had thought.

Pain mixed with disappointment, disbelief, and dread.

Just when she thought she could find some peace at the end of her day, she was bombarded with this message. She realized that if she hadn't snooped, Abdullah would've just added it to his long list of secrets.

Moments later, she heard the key turn in the door. Abdullah walked in. "Asalamu alaikum," he said, his usual calm self, pausing at the counter. Fatina sandwiched her hands between her thighs, pressing on the wound. "Hey, what's going on? Omar gave you a hard time?"

She nodded repeatedly, biting her bottom lip as her eyes filled with tears. Her jeans were stained with blood. Abdullah dropped to his knees, frantically scanning her body. "Fatina, where's this blood coming from!?"

He pulled her hands free, noticed the cut, and quickly grabbed a kitchen towel from the counter to wrap her finger.

"I didn't try to kill myself..." she said, her breath coming in short bursts.

"You're acting strange." He scanned her face. "What happened?"

"I read one of your secret messages," she said, her voice trembling.

Abdullah stared at Fatina for a moment, then reached for the phone, releasing her wrapped hand. His gaze flicked up and down the screen. He opened the back of his phone, removed his SIM card, snapped it in half, and flung the phone across the floor.

"Your finger needs stitches. Come on, I'll help you get dressed so we..."

"I don't care," Fatina said, taking a step back.

Abdullah stepped closer, focused on the blood seeping through the towel, reaching out to help.

"You think this message means shit to me? I've never responded to any of her..."

His voice, shaking with anger, suddenly stopped as he realized his mistake.

"To any of her other messages? She wants to be part of your world!" Fatina shouted, twisting violently out of his reach as her rage intensified. "Your kindness is unprecedented to her, and yes, it means a lot of things, Abdullah!"

Fatina had learned not to ask questions about Abdullah's military activities. But what was this woman's connection to him? She deserved to know everything.

Abdullah backed away, leaning against the wall. His hands were blotched with blood. "Fatina, do I look like a teenager to you? I'm sorry you had to read that. Nothing is going on."

"Then what does this message mean? She's a writer, isn't she? I know exactly who she is! And you've obviously helped her, or saved her from a tragedy, and she's never felt loved."

The towel slipped as she raised her arms, causing blood to drip down. She covered her face with both hands, smearing blood across her cheeks.

***

Fatina woke to find herself in bed. Abdullah lay beside her, deeply asleep, his face nuzzled into her pillow. The last thing she remembered was Abdullah carrying her and putting her abaya on her. They were going to the hospital, but she couldn't recall anything else. A tremor of fear fluttered through her. She shook Abdullah's shoulder.

Then it all hit her at once. The messages. *To be part of your world. Your kindness…* She pictured another woman sleeping with her husband.

Abdullah slightly lifted his head before resting it back on the pillow. "It's all right, habibti. Go back to sleep," he mumbled.

She got up to get some water. In the kitchen, Abdullah had cleaned up the mess. Thoughts of what had happened pressed in on her, but she felt heavy and numb, her body unable to respond. Tomorrow would be another day. She went back to sleep.

Chapter 24

Abdullah: A Talk

When Abdullah woke up the next day, the kids were already up. He showered and made breakfast for them. Habiba ran to her dad and hugged him.

"I missed you, Baba."

Habiba always made him feel better. She was like a sunflower that pushed the gloominess out of his life.

"I came in early last night, but you had already gone to sleep."

"I waited in bed and read a story. I heard Mama shouting." She looked up at him, waiting for reassurance. Then she gathered her courage and said, "Mama is scary sometimes."

"Mama cut herself while making a salad, but she's okay." He squeezed Habiba again. "Sometimes she gets upset about things. Come on, see if Omar needs any help, and let's eat. I'm hungry."

The three of them sat down together to eat hummus and falafel. Abdullah felt grateful for the blessings he had. He thought about the dozens of other kids who had amputations after being shot during the March. It didn't make Omar's situation any easier, but he'd teach him to be strong. He'd keep encouraging him to play on the paraplegic football team. He'd ensure Omar grew up confident.

"I'm taking you to school today," Abdullah said.

Omar didn't protest. He wheeled himself to get ready.

When Abdullah returned after dropping off Omar, Fatina was sitting up in bed.

"Good morning," he said, bending down to kiss her.

"Did I pass out last night?"

Abdullah tucked himself in beside her. "Sort of. They stitched up your finger and gave you something to help you sleep in the ambulance."

"The ambulance? What a way to end last night's drama," Fatina said, her voice tired.

Abdullah decided that, although Dalia's story had to remain secret, Fatina deserved answers.

"I got some *manakeesh*. You want breakfast in bed?" He brushed a strand of hair from her face.

"Abood, please tell me what happened last night was only a bad dream." Fatina leaned against Abdullah's shoulder.

"Listen, that woman has a story. She was involved in something dangerous and needed help getting out. Her life was on the line. She has kids, and she feared losing them. She did some bad things, but she's been cleared now."

"A…spy?" Fatina sucked in a sharp breath.

"Like I said, she was involved in unethical activities. I'm only telling you this so you're reassured. No word of this must get out."

"And you were… helping her."

"She turned to us—me and someone we had assigned to follow her. We knew she was caught up in something, and we stepped in at the right moment. Everybody deserves a second chance, don't you think?"

"But she's still very bold... She literally proposed to you."

Fatina was avoiding looking at Abdullah. But he could see the sallow bags beneath her eyes that revealed a weariness deeper than a lack of sleep.

"You've really worked yourself up over this," he said softly. "I've never paid attention to her. It hurts to know you keep doubting my intentions. And you'll be happy to know I've quit the writers' club."

Fatina untangled herself and went to take a shower.

Abdullah knew she didn't doubt his fidelity, but she feared that woman would lure him. The last thing she needed was more insecurity.

Chapter 25

Masood: No Remorse

Since the night he sat with Dalia, Masood had realized that his sister was getting cold feet. He'd wait and see if she could make a breakthrough now that he'd managed to stir up her fears. At the same time, he'd oversee this operation himself.

Officer Eyad would chew him out for the lack of progress. It wasn't the humiliation Masood feared; it was the threats. Would the officer really blackmail him? If he did, it'd mean exposing others, too. But he couldn't take the chance. He needed to please Officer Eyad.

Masood took a long drag on his fifth cigarette of the day as he walked down the street. A job like this required thick skin, so he'd get the help he needed.

Adnan was waiting for him at the apartment and let him in. The six-floor apartment was a two-bedroom. The entrance led into a fair-sized sitting room and a small open-plan kitchen. Eight plastic chairs were scattered around a grimy table, where a few mugs still held coffee dregs. The air was stale, and Masood twitched his nose.

"It smells like shit in here," he said to Adnan, who made sure the curtains stayed closed as he slid the window open a crack. "We need to move out of here. We've been here too long."

Adnan was in his late thirties, just like Masood. Tall and heavily built, he towered over Masood. His face was stern and gruff, marked by a scar across his left cheek. "What's going on?" he asked.

"Eyad wants Abdullah. He says to interrogate him and report back before we decide how to deal with him," Masood said. "Get the van ready."

Without a word, Adnan went into one of the rooms and returned with a small toolbox. "I'll prepare something special for Abdullah," he said, rubbing the metal lid without opening it.

An uneasy chill swept over Masood. Only Adnan had a box like that. He used it against targets and operatives who failed to accomplish their missions.

"Too bad your sister isn't doing a good job," Adnan said, still admiring the metal box. Then he shifted his gaze to Masood. "I haven't seen her in a while. She'll owe me one after I do her job for her."

***

Masood got to the beach at 4:30 a.m. He'd seen Abdullah run there before and guessed he might show up again. The spot was near the port, an area that became lively around noon. That's when, depending on the weather, people would come to sit and relax. There were also small huts for the fishermen, along with boats, nets, and a few cafés scattered along the shoreline.

But now, it was the darkest hour before the dawn. Masood hid behind one of the fishermen's huts and waited, sitting on the ground. He'd grown weary of these duties, remembering what had entangled him in this kind of work.

Yara.

He had gotten to know Yara online. She'd sent him a Facebook invitation three years ago. Pornographic images of herself soon followed, and he went mad. He wanted to see more of her.

She then asked him a few questions about some people from different political factions. He gave her more than she asked for. She was pleased with him and sent him a handsome sum of money. Masood was shocked. He wanted more. What had he done? He'd only relayed information that was probably common knowledge.

One day, after a meeting with Yara, a political figure Masood had leaked information about was killed by an Israeli drone while he was driving. She asked what kind of car he drove, and Masood gave the license plate number. That was all that was needed.

As the days passed and the money accumulated, Masood became crazier, dared more risks. He cared only about money. Eventually, Yara revealed her true identity. She told him she was an Israeli intelligence officer and threatened to blackmail him if he didn't keep working with her.

The amount of money plummeted. They had him by the throat.

"We have videos of you picking up the money, Masood. All the chats are here. So, it's in your best interest to keep cooperating," the bitch had said.

Masood didn't turn to anyone for advice or help, but he knew the dreadful fate of all the agents who were discovered.

The sun's glare jolted Masood awake. He sprang up, realizing he'd fallen asleep. He would tell Adnan that Abdullah hadn't come to the beach today.

Adnan was nasty. He might have had someone tail him. He hated how Adnan acted like his boss just because he was assigned the more lethal duties. If it weren't for all the spying and information-gathering Masood did so diligently, Adnan wouldn't be able to do his job. Deep down, he knew the Israeli officers didn't favor or value one agent over another. Maybe they paid Adnan more…

The following day, Masood went to a different spot on the beach. He made sure to take Tramadol to stay alert. He couldn't imagine functioning without his pills. It was close to 6 a.m. when people started to appear. A few women were strolling along, some in pairs and others with their husbands. This wouldn't be easy.

Eventually, he spotted two figures jogging along the beachfront. He tugged his cap lower over his eyes and climbed the sand hill until he reached the pavement. Hands in his pockets and eyes scanning the road, Masood ambled in the opposite direction from the two men. He recognized one of them. Pressing the button on his earpiece, he notified the others. "He's here."

It would only take a few minutes for them to get there, but he didn't want to lose Abdullah. The black, tinted-glass van arrived, parked on a side street, and waited. Masood saw Adnan step out of the van and cross the street toward him. They began walking. "The one in the black tracksuit," Masood said.

Abdullah and his friend were getting closer. Adnan looked at Masood, pretending to be completely engaged in conversation. He bumped into Abdullah, who staggered. Adnan moved without hesitation, smoothly jabbing the needle into Abdullah's arm. He always succeeded on the first try.

The van was now parked at the curb. The doors slid open, and they shoved Abdullah inside. Masood pushed the other man onto his back. Even as he fell, the man drew a Glock .42 and fired. Masood shrieked, but Adnan hauled him into the van. The man shot at the tires, but the van swerved away.

Chapter 26

Fatina: Painting

It was daybreak, and Fatina wanted to seize the early morning hours.

Her parents had always been early risers. They'd stay up after Fajr prayer, have breakfast and coffee. Her mother did most of the strenuous housework during those hours. Of course, Fatina herself never joined in their morning ritual, preferring to go back to sleep. Now, as a parent, she had started mirroring her mother's habits, finishing the tidying and cooking first thing in the morning.

This afternoon, she would meet with Tala and Safa to discuss their artists' workshop project. After years of neglect, Fatina decided to revive her passion for drawing and painting. She'd have exhibitions, train young artists, and, if she could keep up her energy, imagined selling her work to people outside Gaza.

Abdullah was unconvinced at first. But when she finally committed to the idea, he picked her up and twirled her around as she giggled. Fatina's laughter brought in Omar and Habiba, who ran to Abdullah and asked to be tossed in the air.

"Did you know that writers and artists complement each other?" he asked.

"How so?"

"They both produce beauty that changes people's lives—like the horse painting you were working on when we met. I can help you market your work," Abdullah said.

"In the battlefield?" she laughed.

Whenever Abdullah mentioned the horse painting, a tide of memories washed over Fatina. The stationery shop near her school. The zeal for painting that had possessed her.

What she missed most about being a teenager was that, back then, she wasn't burdened by responsibilities and hadn't yet seen the complicated puzzle pieces of life. She had lived her youth to the fullest without worrying about what was going on around her. Even growing up under occupation hadn't been her biggest concern—she'd been born into it and had survived it alongside her brothers.

After Fatina's injury, Abdullah had often begged her to return to painting, but she repeatedly refused. Accepting that she had only one good hand wasn't easy. Art is about beauty, and she felt far from it. But now, here she was, meeting with her friends to plan a workshop in Tala's garden. It would be the perfect setting and cost them very little.

By indulging herself, Fatina discovered that her anxieties felt less aggravating. During difficult moments, she retreated to her easel and painted her worries away. There was something about holding a paintbrush and pouring her emotions onto the canvas.

Fatina was also happy to see her son taking an interest in her art. He even agreed to join her at the workshop to try drawing. The fact that he was finally open to doing something with her felt like a promising sign.

Lately, Fatina often lost herself in sketching or outlining new pieces in the evenings, unable to pull herself away even when Abdullah came home. One evening, as she sat before a fresh canvas, he came up behind her and gently caressed her neck.

"I'm jealous," he said.

"I know I spend more time with my paintbrush than with you, but you said I needed a good distraction," Fatina said.

"You're quite distracted," Abdullah admitted.

His admission didn't deter Fatina. She turned around, her face lighting up. "I can draw covers for your future books!"

She had stopped holding back, leaning into every opportunity. Before long, Fatina and her group began receiving commissions to paint murals. Working on them was liberating. When she saw the grand designs come to life on the walls, her spirits lifted, and she felt a rush of joy.

The art form was integral to Palestinian culture. Since she was a little girl, she had seen murals and graffiti on walls. They were the people's way of resisting the occupation, making announcements, and leaving messages, all with affordable spray paint. Artists painted on happy and sad occasions. A greeting for a groom. A farewell to a martyr. Her school had several murals on the walls, both inside and outside the playground. They were occasionally whitewashed and replaced with new works.

When her kids were younger, Fatina once walked in to find them scribbling all over a wall in their bedroom. When she admonished them, Habiba replied, "But everybody writes on the walls outside, Mama." She was speechless.

It was just one example of how parenting in Gaza came with its own set of contradictions. Another time, Omar came home from school and told her that a teacher had called a student a donkey for getting paint on a desk, which he couldn't understand since there was art everywhere. She could only say, "Grown-ups sometimes make mistakes too, habibi."

Back on the couch after her meeting, Fatina paused at the sound of incessant buzzing. She was reading a collection of Mahmoud Darwish's poems, admiring their eloquence.

Set me, if ever I return,

In your oven as fuel to help you cook,

On your roof as a clothesline stretched in your hands.

Weak without your daily prayers,

I can no longer stand.

I am old

Give me back the stars of childhood

That I may chart the homeward quest

Back with the migrant birds

Back to your awaiting nest

Writing was an art form she felt incapable of producing. Whenever she needed to pour out her feelings, she turned to painting. Yet with the same passion, she cherished reading poetry. It felt intimate, comforting. Somehow, the words quieted the turmoil within.

The buzzing continued, snapping her out of her thoughts. Fatina grew tense whenever she heard an aircraft overhead. Even a door slamming made her jump because it sounded like an explosion. She had to get her mind off the aircraft, but she was afraid to wear her earbuds. She needed to hear her surroundings.

Maybe painting would help her relax. Fatina wandered into Abdullah's office, which doubled as her mini art studio. Before she began painting, her mood usually determined what kind of image she would create. Maybe a vast green field with sheep. The shepherd would be content. What more could anyone want than to live in a borderless land?

Just as she reached for the paint in the cabinet, a loud explosion shook the windows of the house. The paint tubes fell from her hands, and she dashed out of the room. Omar and Habiba were in the living room watching TV. They looked to their mother for guidance.

Noticing Fatina's discomfort, Habiba jumped up and ran to her. "It sounds far away, Mama, right?"

Fatina's face went cold, and her stomach cramped. She settled on the couch beside the kids, trying to compose herself. Listening for another explosion, she heard only silence. Her right leg bounced as she pressed her hands between her knees, the nervous energy impossible to shake off.

The news channel on her WhatsApp announced: *The sound heard across Khan Younis was a sonic boom caused by Israeli warplanes over the sea.*

It was their game to terrorize the population with horror from above.

She wondered how Abdullah was. It was the second day he hadn't been home. He always told her if he was going to be away, but this time, Hamza had informed her. He said Abdullah was okay and that something had come up. This filled Fatina with unease. If there was an emergency, it meant the Resistance was preparing to respond to an impending attack.

What if something happened to him? What if he ended up martyred? Would she be as strong as the other wives of martyrs? She'd seen countless mothers and wives bid their loved ones farewell, but it brought her no comfort.

She was astonished by their steadfastness. The way they kissed their men or their children goodbye. The way they pledged to avenge their killing. The way they vowed to carry their legacy. When she asked Abdullah about their resolve, he'd tell her that Allah fills them with patience and solace.

The waiting drained Fatina. She kept herself busy from morning till night. Her routine consisted of household chores, helping the kids with their studies, and bringing them along to her art-related events. In Abdullah's absence, she felt a void and a strong need to keep the children close. Abdullah's mother was at her sister's, leaving Fatina alone in the building.

Pretty soon, it would be dark. She got up, packed some clothes, got the kids ready, and headed to her parents' house.

Chapter 27

Abdullah: Abduction

Abdullah's head throbbed, though he didn't know why. He tried to lift his hand, but it felt as if someone were pressing it down. He couldn't move his body. A strong, foul odor hit his nose, making him nauseous. He jerked forward and vomited. The retching threw him off balance, and he collapsed face-first. His surroundings were dark, except for a dim light in the distance. He strained to listen and heard footsteps approaching.

"What happened, big boy?" a husky voice asked.

Abdullah grasped the horror of the situation he was in. The figure knelt and hissed in his ear, "Abdullah, the freedom fighter." A taunting snicker.

Two big hands set the chair upright. A heavily-built man wearing a balaclava stood in front of him. He jerked Abdullah's head back by the hair and hissed, "Let me lay out the rules of our game. I ask, you answer. Simple enough?"

Abdullah's throat was raw from the bitter, acidic taste of vomit. He didn't reply. The man held a glass of water. Abdullah stared, desperate. But instead of letting him drink it, the man splashed the water in his face. Abdullah gasped as his body shivered.

The man paced back and forth, then stopped again in front of Abdullah. "First question is an easy yes or no. Do you work in the Resistance?"

Abdullah was still trying to figure out how he had ended up wherever he was. He had been jogging with Salem at the beach. That was all he remembered.

He didn't respond.

His interrogator circled behind Abdullah and yanked his head back by the hair again, even more violently than before. "Don't make me repeat questions, you bastard!"

Abdullah thought of freed prisoners who had served time in Israeli prisons. Some could fool the interrogating officers, while others couldn't withstand the torture. But he wasn't in an Israeli prison. Even if the guy was a spy, he probably had the IQ of a child, unlike the intellectual spies depicted in movies. Palestinian spies were mostly driven by money, and their employers didn't provide them with training courses.

"I'm a writer," Abdullah managed to say through short breaths.

The man slapped him across the face and barked, "Lying bastard! Give me the names of your regiment!"

"Water," Abdullah gasped.

"Speak first," the man spat.

Despite his physical collapse and mental strain, Abdullah began to formulate a plan.

"Give me water first," he said without looking at his captor.

As the man motioned for someone else to bring water, Abdullah scanned the room. The two men were holding him in what appeared to be a storage space. Torn pieces of sponge lay strewn across one end of the room. He heard dogs barking outside.

The second man approached with a bottle of water. "Now I have to put it to his mouth like a baby," he scoffed. He raised the bottle, and Abdullah felt life return to him in trickles.

"There's a regiment called Ahmed Faraj," Abdullah said. "It's named after the martyr. Another is called Omar Abdulwahid, also named after a martyr. I once interviewed one of their members for a story I wrote about Resistance fighters."

The two men exchanged glances, and the taller one went off. "This is bullshit! I'm asking about your regiment, the…"

"I told you I don't work in a regiment," Abdullah said.

Knuckles slammed into the side of Abdullah's head, just above his ear. A dull numbness spread across one side of his face, and everything went black. When he began to come to, he kept his eyes closed.

"If you keep beating him up, he won't be able to talk," Abdullah heard one man say.

"Have you heard of those names he mentioned?" the other man asked.

"Yeah. Their pictures hang in the streets."

Abdullah didn't want his life to end at the hands of these scumbags.

A vision of his grandfather appeared before him. "Habibi, you and your generation will liberate our land and return to it," he said. "I'm too old to face the occupation."

Abdullah was profoundly attached to his grandfather. In his dreams, he saw him holding his cane and waiting at the frontier, or tending his trees in a wide, open landscape. He often imagined his grandfather watching from above, trusting Abdullah to carry the same dying wish passed down through generations: to free their homeland.

Chapter 28

Salem: The Chase

Salem jumped on his motorbike and followed the van. It was still visible from a distance, but he feared losing it. He released the clutch and gunned the engine. The back of the van swung open, and he knew exactly what was coming next.

He dodged the bullets by swerving left, then got back on the road while keeping a safe distance from the vehicle. He watched the van veer onto a narrow, sandy road. At the corner, a sign advertised the Paradise Chalet. When he reached the sandy stretch, the van had disappeared.

Gaza was small. Even if these guys didn't have a large network, Salem would still be able to find them.

Everything happened too fast, but he tried to piece together the split-second chaos. Abdullah hadn't fought back and had lost consciousness after the man bumped into him. They had probably injected him with a powerful sedative. If the men wanted to, they could have shot him on the spot. Abducting him meant they were handing him over to someone else.

When they shoved Abdullah into the van, Salem noticed pieces of foam scattered across its floor. He called Bilal and told him to meet him at the beach.

"Bring a couple of snacks with you," Salem added. He knew Bilal would immediately understand that he wasn't asking for breakfast, but for backup.

"I'll bring falafel and hummus. See you soon," Bilal said.

Fifteen minutes later, Bilal and three other men met Salem. Salem turned off his phone and buried it in the sand. He stumbled over his words, speaking rapidly.

"Abdullah has been kidnapped. They abducted him in a van. I followed as best as I could. We need a plan." Salem took a breath, then continued. "There were pieces of foam in the van. Is there a foam factory around?"

The three men stood in stunned silence. Then Bilal said, "Come on. Hop in the car."

The crew searched every chalet in the area. Eight hours yielded nothing. Salem knew who to contact. He called Dalia. She picked up immediately.

"Hey, it's Salem from the writers' club. Did you get the new books?"

Chapter 29

Abdullah: Interrogation

ABDULLAH HAD FALLEN ASLEEP again. He wasn't sure how long he had been out, but he awoke to the murmur of voices.

"We need to get something useful out of him before tomorrow," one man said—meaning they wouldn't kill him today. This gave Abdullah a brief sense of relief.

They walked over to where Abdullah was still tied to the chair. His arms ached. He struggled to figure out how to free himself. He'd seen it done so many times in movies, but this was real life.

"Abdullah, Abdullah, Abdullah. I hear you have a gorgeous wife…" the tall, heavy man began, folding his arms across his chest.

Abdullah's brows furrowed, and cold rage coursed through him. "Don't mention my wife with your filthy tongue, *ya kalb*!" Abdullah roared.

The other man tried to reassure his colleague. "Let's not upset Abdullah. He's a good boy, and he'll give us more information. Won't you, Abdullah?"

Abdullah was worked up but tried to regain his composure. "I told you what I know. Those two regiments are the ones people talk about. They say Ahmed's regiment or Omar's."

"And which regiment are you part of?" the scrawnier one asked.

"I was part of Omar's," Abdullah said. "I worked with Omar when he was alive, but my work was negligible. He was a narcissistic bully, and when I couldn't take his shit anymore, I quit. He never let me in on anything… always made me doubt myself."

The men listened intently, and Abdullah prayed that his story sounded convincing. For a moment, he was grateful that he read mysteries and thrillers.

"What kind of tasks did he give you?"

Abdullah shifted in his seat before answering. "He said the first month was a trial period. I had to prepare food and handle logistics. I drove back and forth all day, bringing in supplies. They made sure I never saw their faces while I was completely exposed. That's how they treat newbies," he finished in disgust.

"Maybe they didn't know your worth, Abdullah. How about working with someone who will promote you from day one?"

The conversation was moving in the right direction.

Abdullah fixed his gaze on the floor and asked, "Is this how you treat people before you decide to hire them?"

Silence stretched across the room, and Abdullah wondered if his snark had caught them off guard. Then the bigger one spoke. "This is the testing part. If you pass the next test, you're hired."

"What kind of test?" Abdullah asked.

"Let's just say it's more delicate than this," the shorter one replied. "You'll need to clean yourself up."

Chapter 30

Dalia: A Test

AFTER SHE CONFESSED to Abdullah, Dalia had felt a surge of blood through her veins. It was like inhaling oxygen that revived her soul. She imagined herself living a normal life again, going to work, and providing for her kids, free from the worry of being called on to seduce men and ruin their reputations and honor. She still feared the possible consequences, but she couldn't turn back. It was the first time she had felt heard or believed she might get another chance.

The days that followed were exhausting—questions, long silences, more questions, and rooms where the walls seemed to press in on her.

When intelligence finally finished interrogating Dalia, she was acquitted of her crimes because they didn't involve killing anyone. At the time, Salem had reminded her to keep tricking Masood into believing she was still playing along until they found the right moment to capture him. She was careful not to let Masood suspect anything.

She had also learned not to ask questions over the phone.

"Yes, the new books came in yesterday. I'll bring them now," Dalia had casually replied when Salem called her.

When she arrived at the club, a janitor was methodically mopping the hallway. Salem was already at the library, standing by the window. As soon as he heard her, he turned and motioned her over to the table.

Salem and his work continued to fascinate Dalia. After her interrogation, she admitted to him that his role as a college student had fooled her. Her impression and attitude toward him changed. Now that she knew the truth, she could see him clearly.

In Salem, she noticed traits and qualities the men in her life lacked: inquisitive eyes, a serious face, measured gestures. Her ex was a greedy, spoiled narcissist who cared only about himself, and her brother was a treacherous agent. As she set the books on the table, Dalia daydreamed for a few seconds about what it would be like to have a real man in her life.

"Is your brother around?" Salem began.

"He's been out since yesterday and hasn't come home."

"One of our men has been kidnapped. This is the work of Israeli intelligence. I need you to tell your brother that you're making real progress in ensnaring Abdullah and that he replied to your messages."

"Who was kidnapped?" she lowered her voice, afraid to hear herself ask.

"Abdullah."

Dalia covered her mouth in disbelief. "Oh no! You think this is Masood's work?"

"He's the prime suspect, of course." Salem's eyes flicked toward the coatroom. "Your phone's ringing."

"Oh, thank you. I didn't even notice," Dalia said, still reeling from his words. She stepped over to the coatroom, dug her phone out of her bag, and answered.

"*Marhaba*. I'm picking you up at 9:00. I have a surprise for you."

It was Masood.

Dalia's heartbeat quickened. She tried to steady her voice. "I hope it's a good one," she said, her tone light but cautious.

"I've done your homework for you. Now you just have to add the final touches," Masood said sternly.

"I'll be ready." She pressed her hand to her chest, knowing a heavy task awaited her.

Putting her phone back in her bag, Dalia returned to the library and repeated what Masood had said.

"I'll have my men follow."

Dalia's face flushed. Overcome with shame and nerves, her voice dropped to a whisper. "What am I going to do?"

"We'll be right behind you," Salem reassured her.

"You don't understand. He's not alone. Some filthy men work with him. They'll kill me if they suspect anything."

"Do you know any of them?"

"Adnan. They call him Poison." Dalia clenched her fists.

"Just try to act normal. You know, business as usual. And, Dalia? Be careful."

"*Shukran.*" With that, Dalia left.

She'd visit the hairdresser first, then the perfume shop, so anyone following her would think she was getting ready for her mission. But she resolved not to let them drag her into the filthy pit again.

Chapter 31

Abdullah: Rescue

"I'm going to untie your arms and take you to a room. There's a shower and some food. But if you try anything, I'll blast your brains out," the taller man said.

Abdullah knew they wouldn't kill him. They needed him. Hiring him would make them look good in front of the Israeli officer they were trying to impress.

They led Abdullah into a small room. The door locked behind him. He checked his pockets; his gun, keys, and wallet were gone. The dank smell repulsed him. The room was empty, save for a twin bed in the far-right corner and a small table with two chairs on the opposite side. A high window near the ceiling was bolted shut. The place was some sort of warehouse.

A pair of sweatpants and a shirt lay on the bed. They'd called it "a delicate task." Panic gripped him. Abdullah knew the depraved techniques agents used to implicate people in espionage.

He released a shuddering breath before opening the bathroom door. The shower tiles were stained with limescale, and the floor was dry. A few long strands of hair clung to the drain.

After showering, Abdullah still felt unclean and nauseous.

Two loaves of saj bread and three small plates—one with white cheese, another with za'atar, and the third with olive oil—were on the table. He had no appetite, but he needed the energy. Just as he was finishing, someone knocked on the door and turned the handle. Abdullah glanced up, the last piece of bread still halfway to his mouth.

Dalia came in, closed the door behind her, and sat in the chair opposite.

Abdullah remained silent for a few seconds. He needed to be careful with his words.

"So, you're the delicate task," he said loudly, scanning the room for hidden cameras. His voice rising, he spoke directly to the men, knowing they were watching, "If you think I'm doing this while you pigs are watching, you'd better think again."

Dalia's face contorted in horror. Her hands trembled as she fixed her attention on the leftover food. Abdullah leaned back, his arms folded. Within seconds, the skinny man entered the room.

"What's all the fuss, Abdullah?" he asked.

"If you want me to do this, I'll do it my way," Abdullah said, avoiding eye contact.

The man looked at Dalia, then back at Abdullah, and sneered. "So, you two have met before… you're familiar with each other."

At that exact moment, Salem and five other men were positioned behind the warehouse, as Abdullah would later learn.

Salem's suspicions were confirmed: it was a foam warehouse. It was also one of those times when living on such a small piece of land felt like a blessing. No highways or long distances separated cities or villages, so putting together the puzzle pieces had been more manageable.

Salem noticed several windows that were too high to reach. Two guards flanked a two-meter-wide metal door. Given the minimal security measures, the warehouse was likely a temporary operational base.

Exactly 90 seconds later, the electricity went out.

The men made their move. Bilal struck one of the guards with the butt of his rifle. At the same time, Salem took out the other man and slid the door open.

"Farouq, isn't the generator on automatic?" a voice called out.

Salem aimed, the silencer on his gun muffling the shot, and kept moving. The entire six-man crew, including Bilal, stormed the warehouse.

Inside the room with Abdullah and Dalia, Masood quickly realized he'd been caught. He spun around, grabbed Dalia by her hijab, and pressed his gun to her temple. Dalia gasped and let out a sharp, panicked scream.

Abdullah saw her open her palm and bring a small tube to her mouth. "Dalia, no! Don't!" he screamed.

"You treacherous bitch!" Masood snatched her head back.

"Run, Abdullah!" Dalia shouted before collapsing.

The door of the room flew open, and Abdullah came face-to-face with Salem and the others. Masood aimed a gun at Abdullah with a shaky grip. In one swift motion, Abdullah snatched the chair behind him and flung it at his face. Masood yelled as the gun slipped from his grasp.

"Call an ambulance!" Abdullah shouted to the others. He checked Dalia's pulse—weak but still there.

"The car! Let's go," Bilal said, lifting Dalia and running out of the building.

Masood, half-conscious, tried to recover from the blow.

"This one is mine," Abdullah growled, yanking Masood by the collar and slamming him against the wall. Masood yelped pathetically.

Boiling rage surged through Abdullah, fierce and unrelenting. His fists struck in controlled bursts, each hit a question, a demand for answers, forcing Masood to twist and cover his face.

"You scum! You traitor! You trash!" Abdullah barked, his voice raw with anger as he hurled profanities, punctuating each with short, hard strikes. Masood tried to jab, stumbling backward, but he never landed a blow.

Abdullah's breath came in ragged bursts. Every muscle in his body was coiled, every movement precise as he alternated between relentless punches and smashing Masood's head against the wall. "Tell me, *ya kalb*," he hissed, his chest heaving, "who sent you after me?"

A sharp shout cut through the tension. "This place is bugged! Drones are circling outside! Everybody out—now!" Salem grabbed Abdullah's arm.

Abdullah shoved Masood aside. The agent crumpled against the wall, his face bloodied.

The six men rushed through the warehouse doors and into the night. The last thing Abdullah saw was Salem beside him before the blast hurled them all into the air, slamming them into the bushes below. Behind them, the warehouse erupted in a deafening explosion, fire and smoke billowing skyward.

Chapter 32

Fatina: Restless

FATINA HAD BEEN ASLEEP when she heard the explosion. She bolted out of bed, clutching her chest as her pulse raced. "Abdullah…" she murmured to herself.

The blast also woke Habiba, who came running to her. Fatina rubbed her back. "It's okay, habibti," she said.

"Mama, you're shaking," Habiba said.

"I'm…cold," Fatina lied. A few moments later, another fear-induced chill ran through her body.

"Mama, is there going to be a war?" Habiba asked sleepily.

Fatina felt a deep ache. The world her kids were born into and grew up in was shaped by war. Sometimes she liked to think they would be stronger than she was.

Fatina had also grown up under occupation, but her brothers had empowered her. They told her that Israeli soldiers were sissies, and for a long time, she didn't fear them at all. But then the aerial shelling began. As she realized a warplane could strike at any time—day or night—and bomb a house, a car, or any place at the press of a button, life became unbearably precarious. When she witnessed young men being butchered by Israeli missiles from above, as in 2008, she experienced a new kind of terror.

On that late December afternoon, she was at home, enjoying what felt like a quiet moment. Then, without warning, explosions rocked the area. Her TV screen showed a slaughterhouse scene: police cadets targeted during their graduation ceremony. It was all the confirmation she needed that the entire occupation army was bloodthirsty and cowardly—an unpredictable combination.

"No. Insha'Allah, we won't see any more wars," she said as she lay down beside her daughter, slowly calming her thudding heart. She drifted back to sleep, a drone's buzzing disturbing her rest.

A few hours later, Fatina woke again. She listened closely. The shelling had stopped, but the drone's sound still rang in her ears. She immediately remembered dreaming of seeing Abdullah at... the same place where Omar was rushed after he was shot!

Fatina gently let go of Habiba, pulled her abaya off the hanger on the back of the door, and slipped out of the room.

In the living room, her father was reciting the Quran while praying Fajr. His voice had always been a source of comfort. She didn't read the Quran as often as her father, but she loved listening to his recitation.

When they were kids, Fatina and her brothers would gather around as their father told them Quranic stories. Like any child, Fatina was captivated by narratives. She fixated on her father's every action. His words, his movements, and the way he carried each story brought everything to life for her, helping her grasp the meaning behind them.

Fatina remembered feeling scared and heartbroken after learning that the Prophet became an orphan at the age of six. She often interrupted her dad with questions. "Baba, how did Prophet Muhammad live without his mother and father?"

"His uncle, Abu Talib, raised him. He loved him dearly," her father told her.

Fatina had still shuddered at the thought of losing a parent, but it comforted her to know that the Prophet was loved by his uncle. Her father reassured her that Allah sends loving people to care for you.

At the end of each week, Fatina and her brothers would sit on a floor mattress, and their mother would serve them tea and cake. Her father would hold competitions between them to see who could memorize a particular chapter of the Quran first. She had won a few times. Despite living under occupation, somehow nothing interrupted the weekly gatherings. The most memorable thing about family nights was how peaceful they were.

She yearned for those childhood stories and moments of togetherness.

Fatina went upstairs to Hamza's apartment and knocked. His wife answered the door. "Ayah, is Hamza here?" Fatina asked.

"No," she said. "I haven't slept since the *qassef*. Come in." Ayah's eyes were red and tired.

Fatina could see that Ayah was no better off than she was. She hugged herself, either from the cold or nervousness.

Ayah and Hamza were the family's epic love story. Hamza met her by chance at a bakery, but the moment he saw her, he knew who she was. Ayah was the widow of his dear friend and fellow Resistance fighter, Riyad, who had been murdered by the occupation. Hamza later told Fatina that meeting Ayah felt like "transcending time and place." In the fleeting seconds their eyes met, he saw not just the melancholy and shame of her circumstances—a widow with an 18-month-old child—but also a glimpse of a shared future.

Their mother had a fit when he announced he wanted to marry an older widow with a child. People talked, advice was given, and tempers flared. But Hamza was passionate and stubborn, convinced that love was worth fighting for, even against societal opinion. Fatina had admired his courage since they were children. Years later, she still remembered what he told his mother: "She's worthy of being loved in a way that only I can. I won't give up on her." And he hadn't.

"Did Hamza tell you anything?" Fatina asked, studying Ayah's face.

Her sister-in-law looked at the ground. "No. He just said not to worry if he's late."

"That's all?" Fatina didn't buy it. She offered Ayah a quick "salam" and bolted down the stairs, holding her abaya up slightly so she wouldn't trip.

The streets were still quiet. It was too early for the usual Friday bustle that would come after *Jummah* prayer. A lone bread and *ka'ak* seller pushed his cart, calling out, "*Ka'ak!*" Some women carried empty baskets on their way to the market. They preferred to buy the meat and vegetables themselves.

Fatina always wondered why they didn't just let their husbands handle those errands. She thought it was either part of their loyalty to the kitchen or that their men didn't know how to buy good vegetables. Palestinian women were particular about the sizes of vegetables. Her mother often scolded her father for buying zucchini or eggplants that were too big for *mahshi*. Fatina was surprised she could conjure up life's small details at such a time.

With hardly any cars on the street at this hour, Fatina kept walking. She quickened her pace, driven by the image from her dream. Her gut told her Abdullah was at the hospital. Although she was focused on the path ahead, Fatina didn't notice anyone. Everything around her seemed to fade. So when someone stepped in front of her, she didn't see him coming.

"Fatina," a voice whispered.

She was face-to-face with Hamza. Panting for breath, she said, "I need to go," as she brushed past him.

Hamza held her elbow lightly. "Come with me," he said.

Fatina stopped and looked him in the face. "What happened? I know you're hiding something."

"I'm taking you to see Abdullah," he said. "He's fine. He was hurt a bit, but he's…"

Fatina's chest heaved. "In the *qassef*?"

Hamza nodded.

"No!"

He led her to a waiting car. Her knees shook, and adrenaline surged through her. They got in and sped towards Nasser Hospital.

Chapter 33

Hamza: Emergency Room

Hamza was about to leave Nasser Hospital after failing to find Abdullah there when the ER erupted into chaos. Ambulance sirens wailed, tires screeched on the asphalt, doctors shouted orders, and screams for help filled the air. Six men were pushed in on stretchers.

Running toward the commotion, Hamza screamed, "Abdullah!" when he spotted him among the injured. He found the ambulance driver and asked what had happened.

"From the *qassef*. We found them in the bushes near the chalets. Two dead," the man told him.

Hamza dashed back inside, adrenaline racing through his veins. Pandemonium reigned as nurses ran to fetch equipment and doctors worked to resuscitate those still alive. Paramedics wheeled two stretchers into the operating room. Hamza examined his comrades' faces.

Hassan and Zafer were dead.

He leaned over Hassan and wailed. His friend's face was charred, and parts of his brain gushed out from the impact of the explosion. Zafer's condition was equally grim; half his face was gone. He kissed each of them on the forehead and bid them farewell.

"I'm sorry, habibi. I'm sorry…" he wept.

They weren't the first comrades he had lost. Many others had fallen before, each with a name, a family, and a legacy he needed to honor. Every time he buried a comrade, the weight of his duty settled more heavily.

Hamza was soon pushed into the corridor. He paced back and forth. Fatina had looked him in the eye, asking about Abdullah, and he had lied to her.

When she arrived at their parents' house with the kids, she had caught him just before he left.

"Hamza, tell me where Abdullah is," Fatina demanded, her face taut. "He's never been gone this long without telling me."

He placed his hands on her shoulders. "Calm down, sis. He's all right. I can't say much. He should be home tomorrow. I can't get in touch with him…"

"I don't understand this excessive secrecy. I've been married to him for how long, and yet I'm treated like this?" She stomped off.

Hamza tried to reason, "Fatina, please. I don't know…"

"Stop saying that," her voice cracked. "You know everything. I'm not asking for a detailed report."

Hamza felt awful. If Abdullah had been on a mission, he would've given his sister an idea of when he was returning home. But he didn't have the heart to tell her that spies had abducted her husband. He needed Fatina to have faith that he was bringing Abdullah home. He'd never let her down in his life, whether it meant beating up boys who harassed her at school or bringing her lunch when she forgot it.

Fatina wasn't backing down, so he left to continue the search without fully reassuring her.

Now, Hamza watched the operating room door swing open and called out, "Doctor!" as he ran.

"They're alive," the doctor said without looking up from his chart.

Hamza blocked his path. The doctor regarded him with weary eyes. Hamza realized this was just another routine moment for doctors, who spoke with patients' families dozens of times each day. But that didn't make it normal. He deserved answers.

"Tell me how they are, please. I'm the one who has to inform their families. There's no one else." Hamza motioned across the waiting area.

"Head, chest, and abdominal injuries. I operated on the one with head trauma," he said, checking his chart again quickly. "Abdullah."

***

It was 4:30 AM when Hamza woke to the sound of the Fajr *adhan*. He'd slept on a metal chair in the corridor. The events of the night hit him all at once, and the chill of the hallway settled into his bones along with them. He stood, rubbing his arms, and approached the reception desk.

"Please, I need to check on my brother-in-law and my other friends," he told the woman at the desk. As he waited for her to answer, he prayed that nothing bad had happened while he was asleep.

The woman picked up a chart. "Their names are Abdullah, Salem…"

"Ibrahim and Izz," Hamza impatiently finished for her.

"Stable condition. They're all still on pain meds," the receptionist said, her eyes returning to her computer screen.

He asked if he could see them, but the answer was a firm no. He needed to find a way to get in. There was no one else on duty except a nurse making his rounds. This shouldn't be hard.

Hamza stepped away, then returned to the reception desk. "Are you…" He glanced at her badge. "Ms. Mona? There's someone calling for you."

Mona knitted her brows, got up, and turned down a hall. Hamza saw the cameras, but he didn't care. He pushed through the Intensive Care Unit door.

Abdullah and Salem were in the same room. The humming and beeping of the medical devices sent a chill through him. They both had tubes in their mouths and IV lines in their arms. He ran to Abdullah, trying to make sense of the screen tracking his vitals. The door opened, and two doctors escorted him out of the room.

"You want him to live or die?" one of them asked, chiding Hamza.

At least he could tell his sister that Abdullah was alive.

Chapter 34

Bilal: Saved

Bilal carried Dalia from the car as he ran toward the ER at Nasser Hospital, shouting, "Help!" He needed to save her. It wasn't Jasmine he was carrying, but he couldn't fail again. He just needed to run faster. His face was drenched in sweat, every nerve alive, fueled by a massive surge of energy.

Before he reached the entrance, two paramedics rolled a stretcher towards him. They pushed it inside, but Bilal kept running after it until they reached the emergency room. "She's poisoned!" Breathless, he handed them the glass tube.

He felt someone grip his shoulder and pull him back. He turned to see Hamza, who tried to calm him. "Get a grip, man. She'll be fine, insha'Allah," Hamza said.

Bilal was disheveled, his face pale. "I have to save her. I can't let her die."

He was delirious. Hamza sat him down and took a seat beside him, but he kept mumbling. "She can't die. No… please, Allah…"

His breathing grew shallow, and his voice faded to a whisper.

The last thing Bilal saw was a nurse approaching him. Seconds later, he was asleep.

When he came to, he was staring at a white ceiling. A small monitor caught his attention before he realized he was in a hospital bed. Daylight streamed through the pulled-up blinds. Somewhat disoriented, Bilal removed the green-and-white covers and changed out of the hospital gown. Everything felt foggy as he tried to jog his memory.

Dalia.

Bilal turned the knob and stepped out of the room. A few people were sitting on the metal chairs in the corridor. He stopped a passing nurse to ask about Dalia. Glancing at his watch, he quickly calculated, "I brought her in late last night, around 11:30."

The nurse walked over to the reception desk and pulled out a chart. "Dalia Rihan? Poisoning?"

"Yes, yes." Bilal leaned on the counter, trying to read it. His stomach tightened into a knot.

The nurse drew the chart back slightly, raising an eyebrow. "What's your relationship to her?"

"I'm her neighbor. How is she?" Bilal realized it was a stupid thing to say.

"I'm sorry, but only family…"

Digging into his pocket, Bilal fished out his intelligence credential. He flashed it for the nurse to see. She froze for a moment, then said, "She's okay. I'll have to speak with the department head. Please wait."

She hurried away and returned with a middle-aged man in a lab coat. Bilal didn't wait for him to speak. "I'm Bilal from intelligence. I brought in Dalia Rihan. I'm investigating the case and need to see her."

The doctor adjusted the stethoscope around his neck. "Are you alone on this case?" he asked, skeptically.

"I'm not alone. My partner is on his way. The nurse can stay with me until he arrives."

Bilal couldn't explain what had come over him as he carried Dalia to the emergency room. The memory of holding Jasmine in the same position with the same urgency came rushing back. He knew he had to save Dalia. Relief washed over him when the nurse told him she was okay. He had made it in time. Something deep within him settled, a calm and contentment he hadn't felt in years. It was as if a missing piece had quietly returned.

He went inside to see her. She was asleep. The nurse showed Bilal the monitor readings. Trying to sound professional, he told her he needed to be informed immediately when Dalia woke up.

As Bilal left Dalia's room, Hamza was waiting outside. The two looked at each other for a moment that felt too long. Bilal realized he hadn't asked about Abdullah and the others. "What happened?"

"I'll tell you what happened. You were hallucinating about Dalia. I had them give you a sedative."

Bilal felt exposed. "What do you mean? Did I say any…"

"I need to go back to Abdullah and the others," Hamza cut him off. "And to answer your second question, yes, you were saying things."

Bilal rubbed the back of his neck and stared blankly ahead, trying to process his feelings. But this wasn't the time or place. He and Hamza walked together to the intensive care unit to check on their comrades.

Chapter 35

Abdullah: Alive

WHY WAS IT SO HARD to open his eyes? It felt as if something heavy were pressing down on his eyelids. He needed to keep trying. He wanted to call out, but his mouth was dry. If Fatina was in bed beside him, why wasn't she helping?

A door squeaked as gentle footsteps approached.

"Abood…" Fatina was crying. He recognized the fragrance on her clothes as she rested her forehead on his arm and kissed it. "Abood, are you okay? Talk to me, please…"

Abdullah couldn't move his lips, but he squeezed Fatina's hand as she held it.

"The doctor gave him sedatives, so he can't respond properly," he heard Hamza explain.

When the doctor came in, he told them their time was up, but Fatina wouldn't budge. "I'm not leaving," she said in a choked voice, gripping Abdullah's arm tightly.

She stayed with him until evening—and then every day for a whole week.

By the time Abdullah was released from the hospital, Salem and the others had already been discharged. Abdullah struggled to remember exactly what had happened the night he caught Masood. He had him, the traitor who went against everything he stood for. He struck mercilessly, each punch a release of the betrayal he'd endured. But then… the world shattered. His memory ended there.

Hamza told him they'd barely escaped in time. As they were running out, a drone hovering over the warehouse attacked them. Hamza also mentioned that Masood was gone.

"You don't need to worry about Masood anymore. His own employers eliminated him."

"What about…" Abdullah rubbed his forehead, trying to summon his memory.

"Dalia," Hamza filled in. "She survived. Let's just say your man Bilal is looking after her." He winked.

Chapter 36

Alya: Back to the March

Staying at her sister Adla's for a while was only an excuse for Alya. She was thankful Abdullah was also away, or he would've interrogated her—asking how long she would stay, telling her she needed to come home, and insisting he missed her. That's also why she made sure to tell him before she left, "I'll only be gone a few days, habibi. I miss my sister."

She enjoyed spending time with her sister, especially after Abu Abdullah's passing. Nobody understood her. They just saw her as an old woman whose elderly husband had naturally passed away. But they didn't grasp that Abu Abdullah meant everything to her.

Amer and Alya. She loved how musical their names sounded when spoken aloud.

Amer was the most handsome man in town. Her father had hired him to work in their lush, expansive garden. Alya would watch him from the balcony as he raised the hoe high before striking the soil. He wore a black sirwal, which became dirt-stained as he worked, and wrapped a keffiyeh around his head to protect it from the sun.

Sometimes Alya would make him tea and leave it on the fountain stone. She'd wait until she could see Amer coming to get it, then, just before he arrived, she'd run up the stairs. Once, when she dared to turn back, she found him standing there, staring at her.

When she and Amer wed, they hosted the party in their front yard. She was just shy of sixteen, and he was twenty. It was the perfect wedding. The henna tattoos. The embroidered wedding dress. The *somaqia*, lovingly made by elderly women as they sang and ululated. Neighbors and friends from nearby villages came. They danced, ate, and sang folksongs.

Henna, especially, held meaning. They had a few henna shrubs in their yard, and Alya watched the entire process of picking, drying, grinding, and turning it into paste. Henna was something every bride welcomed because it was rooted in the land, their Palestinian soil. Everything was grown and made by their own hands.

But girls today didn't want all that. Her own daughter, Amal, was adamant about wearing a fancy wedding gown, which cost a thousand shekels to rent for one night. Then the wedding had to be staged in a *sala*, with loud, modern music that Alya found tasteless. She was happier remembering her own wedding.

Alya's nostalgia was deep, like a sickness. She could still recall every detail and every corner of her home and land. They had grown all kinds of vegetables and fruits, and never needed to go to the market. Whether it was tomatoes, potatoes, cauliflower, lettuce, or *molokhiyya*, everything was readily available. Olive and palm trees marked the boundaries of their land. The lemon and orange trees grew closer to the house.

Her children would never understand the yearning that wracked her.

Abdullah and his family stopped attending the Return March after Omar was shot, but this only pushed Alya to keep going. She knew she couldn't pressure Abdullah into taking her, but ever since she glimpsed the sprawling land beyond the fence, her heart had been captivated. Maybe all it would take was walking a few meters, and she'd reach Al-Majdal. No. She remembered Abu Abdullah saying it was longer than that.

"Yallah, Adla. We have to catch the bus," she said impatiently. "It's parked at the *souk*. Did you fix the baking soda solution?"

Adla patted her bag and smiled. "Everything's in here. I hope we won't need to use it. Let's go."

Adla was Alya's youngest sister. Though she was in her mid-fifties and stronger on her feet, it was Alya who was more powerfully drawn to the March.

Today, as with every protest, Alya had chosen her clothes with care. She again wore a *thobe* she'd embroidered herself. She always felt proud to wear it and show it off. She completed her outfit with a white hijab and carried an oversized Palestinian flag.

The creases around her eyes had deepened since her husband's passing and her son's martyrdom, but her beauty still hinted at a once-alluring young woman.

She missed Mahmoud dearly. Thoughts of him often arrived hand in hand with memories of Amer. One loss seemed to echo the other. Mahmoud was just a year younger than Abdullah. Having only three children wasn't the norm in Palestinian society. She and Amer had tried to have more, but it hadn't worked.

Mahmoud was killed when an F-16 fired a missile at a man riding a motorcycle. He was simply walking nearby. Many were killed when Israelis targeted someone on their list. The bystanders were reduced to collateral damage, adding yet another layer of dehumanization to their lives.

Alya grieved over Mahmoud for weeks, until she felt her heart would stop from sorrow. One night, he visited her in a dream. He was happy, running through a rich green field that had no bounds. He told her, "Yumma, I'm alive." It was as if Allah had sent the dream to soothe her heart.

Linking arms with her sister, Alya trudged along the dirt road. Dozens of people stood scattered about three hundred meters from the separation fence, facing the snipers. The young men, women, and kids hollered chants of, "Allahu Akbar!" Many masked their faces with keffiyehs to hide their identities from the soldiers, yet they were all within the snipers' range.

Alya tightened her hold as she moved in small, steady steps. Her breath grew short, but she persisted. "I don't know if I'm carrying my knees or if my knees are carrying me," she said, laughing, before pressing a hand to her chest.

"Slow down. We have lots of time," Adla reassured her.

After a moment of taking everything in, Alya pointed. "Why don't we get near the fence like those people?"

"Why do you want to do that? We can see fine from here. I can get you a chair, and you can…" Adla started to reply.

"I don't want to sit! I came to get a closer look at our land beyond the fence. Let's go," Alya insisted, dragging her feet forward.

"Alya, our land isn't right beyond the fence," Adla said, raising her voice above the clamor.

A crack of gunfire tore through the air, followed by the shrieks of birds. Adla ducked, but Alya stood tall. "Get down, Alya!"

This happened every Friday at the March, and things always escalated fast.

Streams of people raced away from the fence, their feet pounding like an earthquake. An ambulance sped along the dirt road, kicking up clouds of dust. Two paramedics jumped out and stood over someone, who was then placed on a stretcher. The ambulance whizzed by again, its siren a mournful wail. They'd find out who it was once the news got out. The snipers either shot to kill or to maim for life. Alya had seen amputees return on crutches. They were all youths, but she wouldn't let this deter her.

"Come on, Adla. Don't be scared. They haven't shot any women," Alya said.

"They've shot children! Yallah, let's go back!"

An internal force propelled Alya. Amer had always longed to return to their house in Al-Majdal, and it shattered Alya that he died before his dream could come true. During his final days, he told her where he kept the key to their house and all the ownership documents.

"Alya, guard them with your life," he had said. "You, the children, and the grandchildren will go back. Don't ever give up hope."

With Amer's words echoing in her mind, Alya kept marching. Using the flagpole as a cane, she shuffled forward. Her gait was unsteady, but she was determined to push on. Someone called out to her, "*Hajja*, where are you going?" but she couldn't turn back.

In front of her, the crowd that had regrouped was fleeing from the fence again. Dozens of white smoke swirls billowed down on the protesters. Tear gas. Her eyes stung, and a bitter heat scorched her throat. Alya couldn't see, but she heard screams, chants, and sirens. She pressed her hijab to her nose and mouth, choking on the gas, then collapsed.

Chapter 37

Abdullah: Recuperation

After Abdullah was released from the hospital, he received visitors almost every day. Comrades, his commanding officer, and even one of the movement's senior leaders all stopped by. As far as nosy neighbors, relatives, and acquaintances were concerned, Abdullah was simply under the weather. The true story, with all its details, was kept secret.

Abdullah watched the Ministry of the Interior's press conference, during which the spokesperson announced that two high-profile spies had been killed in the operation. He emphasized that anyone who chose to work for the enemy and abandon their own people has only one place in this world: "the trash heap of history." Yet he urged those who were implicated or coerced into collaborating with the enemy to come forward and confess, so their lives might be spared.

"I implore those who have been misled into becoming agents or gathering information on their fellow Palestinians to stop immediately. We are granting them a thirty-day amnesty period. This is their only chance to begin a new, clean chapter in their lives. Their identities will be protected, and…"

Abdullah was content that Dalia had come to him of her own volition. Although their acquaintance started off on the wrong foot, he was grateful to have played a part in helping save someone's life. She may feel pangs of guilt for the rest of her life, but at least she could walk around safely and raise her kids.

The doorbell rang. Habiba picked up the intercom. A familiar voice answered. "Baba, it's Ammou Bilal," she said, still holding down the intercom speaker button.

Abdullah sat on the sofa, his legs stretched out on the coffee table, with a cushion behind his head. Ever since the attack, headaches had become a daily part of his life. He'd also experience vertigo and nausea at times. The doctors said it would either go away with time or become chronic. At least he was still in one piece.

"Tell him to come up."

A moment later, Bilal stepped inside, slipping off his shoes at the door. "Asalamu alaikum, Abu Omar."

"Walaikum asalam. You can keep your shoes on," Abdullah said, watching Bilal neatly line up his sneakers on the doormat.

"That's what you say, but it's Um Omar's floor. I can also feel my mother watching me." Bilal laughed.

Abdullah tossed the cushion aside and was about to stand to shake hands, but Bilal motioned for him to stay put. "I'm not the king," he said. "How are you feeling today?"

Abdullah had been struggling with anything that required concentration for longer periods of time. "I'm taking the pills," he replied simply.

"When I think of everything that happened, it's unbelievable. We were trying to capture Masood, but they did the job for us," Bilal said.

Abdullah found it hard to respond. Many details of that night had somehow slipped from his memory, which deeply unsettled him. Then there were the nightmares. He would wake up screaming, "Dalia, don't!" When Fatina had to wake him, it only made things worse between them.

Because of his condition, she didn't ask him anything. But as his strength slowly returned, he noticed she was being cool toward him.

Abdullah turned to Bilal, a smile tugging at his lips. "But you didn't come here to talk about that, right?"

"You're impossible!" Bilal exclaimed, flinging his arms in mock despair. "How do you know what you know?"

"I know you inside out, brother," Abdullah teased.

Bilal's expression grew serious as he sat quietly, searching for the right words.

"Take your time, lover," Abdullah said as he turned off the TV. He still couldn't wipe the grin away.

"Sometimes I don't know who I am, or why I act in a certain way… or how my brain works…" Bilal began.

"It's the work of the heart, not the brain," Abdullah replied.

"It all happened when I carried her and ran like a madman to the emergency room. I thought… I mean, I felt like I was holding Jasmine." Bilal paused. "Please tell me I'm not losing my mind."

Abdullah patted Bilal's leg. "You're regaining your heart, believe me. And this time, you've given yourself the chance to be who you truly are."

"Does anyone know… anything about her?" Bilal asked.

"Nobody needs to know anything about her past. She is who she is now," Abdullah said, noticing his friend visibly relax.

"I'd be lost without you, you know that," Bilal said.

"Stop the romance." Abdullah chuckled, and Bilal laughed along until Habiba came in, asking what the joke was.

"Baba, you haven't laughed like that in a long time!" She wrapped her arms around Abdullah's neck and kissed his cheek. Abdullah melted. It was good to feel like himself again.

"You know Ammou Bilal is a funny guy."

As Habiba cheerfully skipped out of the room, he turned back to Bilal, his expression changing. "Take the next step if you're ready," Abdullah said.

"You have to come with me to convince my mother," Bilal replied, drumming his fingers nervously against his leg. "She'll have a fit when she finds out about Dalia's circumstances."

Abdullah first needed to make sure Bilal understood the responsibility. He'd be happy with Dalia, but the package included raising her two kids. It might not be fair for him to shoulder that burden, but it was the price of love.

The two friends continued their conversation.

Chapter 38

Fatina: Portrait

Fatina's phone played relaxing music as she sat drawing in a corner of Abdullah's small office. She needed some time to bring herself to finish his portrait. When she was upset with her husband, she would turn the canvas to face the wall.

Drawing the eyes was the highlight of her work, so she saved it for last. She gently outlined their shape on the canvas with a charcoal pencil. A quiet heat stirred within her, as if she were really tracing Abdullah's eyes with her fingers. She was torn between empathizing with what he had gone through and feeling vexed about being left in the dark yet again.

"You love the guy?" Abdullah asked, quietly watching as he stood behind her. Fatina kept sketching, trying to appear completely engrossed in her artwork.

"I need to focus…" she said, attempting to stay composed.

Abdullah's arms encircled her from behind. She felt numb but didn't push him away. "What do you think of it so far?" she asked.

He lovingly rubbed Fatina's neck. "It's missing something," he said.

Fatina laid down her pencil. "Missing what?"

"Some love," he whispered.

Fatina kept to herself as Abdullah recuperated. She took good care of him but avoided asking questions. Her persistent curiosity about the abduction and its details drove her mad. For her own peace, she'd finally chosen to live in her world of painting and be content with that.

She pushed her chair back and stood. "I need a break," she said, heading for the door, but Abdullah caught her hand.

"Look at me," he said.

"I'm not in the mood…"

"You're not in the mood for me? You're not being fair, Fatina. I don't want you to feel sorry for me. I just want you to understand."

Fatina tilted her head back, then lowered it again as tears shimmered in her vision. "I do understand. You got abducted, and I'm told you were on a mission. That woman's name comes up again, and I can't tell how she figures into all of it. And it's obvious you dream about her."

She clenched her jaw and crossed her arms, blinking hard to keep the tears from spilling. "But guess what?" Her voice trembled as she continued, "I've decided I no longer care about what happened, so you can rest assured I won't be nagging you with any more questions." She swiftly brushed at her cheeks.

Abdullah let out a long breath, his shoulders sinking. "Okay, I owe you an explanation. But be prepared for some nasty details. The only reason I haven't told you is that I didn't want to upset you."

Fatina's phone rang. At first, she ignored it, waiting for Abdullah to continue. But when it kept ringing, she checked the screen. It was Khaltu Adla. She passed the phone to Abdullah. "It's your aunt," she said.

"Hello, Khaltu… tear gas… where?!" Abdullah abruptly ended the call.

"Mama is in the hospital."

He hurried out of the room.

Chapter 39

Abdullah: Nostalgia

It didn't take long for Abdullah to reach the hospital. He paid the taxi driver extra to prevent him from picking up other passengers along the way. He felt a bit dizzy from the rush but tried to stay alert.

Um Abdullah was in the ER with a nasal cannula in place. Khaltu Adla was by her side. As soon as she saw Abdullah, she stood, hugged him, and began to cry.

"The bastards shot tear gas from their jeeps and from those drones," Adla started to explain, tears streaming down her cheeks. "I ran. I thought she was behind me. They fired multiple canisters at once." She finished her frantic story, twirling her finger in the air to mimic the spirals of tear gas.

"It's all right, Khaltu."

Abdullah clasped his mother's hand, his thumb tracing slow, steady circles. It was warm. She was a strong woman. She'd be fine. Still, he couldn't believe she'd outsmarted him by going to the March. He thought she'd put protests behind her after Omar's amputation.

Um Abdullah was back home after two days in the hospital. She didn't know what had happened to Abdullah, and he didn't want to get her worked up. She was lying on the sofa in her small living room when he came in to see her. In one hand, she held *subha* beads; her other hand rested absentmindedly against her right cheek. She didn't notice him when he came in.

Abdullah pulled a chair up beside her and kissed the side of her head. "How are you today, habibti?"

Um Abdullah didn't respond right away. She guided the beads through her fingers while her lips moved in soft remembrance. "I can't wait to be reunited with your father," she said wistfully. "It's my only wish."

"Yumma, what's the matter with you? Stop this talk. Now, are you going to tell me what's really bothering you?"

Um Abdullah leaned back and sighed. "What's there to tell? I promised your father I would carry this key and one day unlock our home with it." She pulled out the key she wore around her neck. "Our stolen house; I know it's still there. I dream about it. I can still smell the fragrance of the almond blossoms, the mango tree, the oranges. I can still feel the cool breeze in our garden… You wouldn't understand, Abdullah."

She paused, inspecting her son's face. "And don't think you can fool me by pretending you're okay. You aren't the right color."

Abdullah fought to stay composed as his mother sank into nostalgia. True, he had never lived in their house in Al-Majdal. But he'd grown up listening to his parents' and grandparents' stories. As a child, he would sit with his siblings and listen carefully as his father and grandfather shared details of home. They called it *al-bilad*—the homeland.

When he was too young to understand the whole story, Abdullah would ask his grandfather, "Why can't we just go back if it's not so far, Siddo?" And his grandpa would reply honestly, "Because they stole our land, and if we tried to go back, they'd shoot us."

Those stories, repeated and passed down, became woven into his being—an inseparable part of who he was. When his grandfather passed, Abdullah was devastated because he had died with a heavy heart. Siddo was never truly happy. He often sat quietly, lost in thought. While he owned a piece of land in Gaza where he planted olive and palm trees, he'd always say, "These trees aren't like the ones we had back home. It's like having foster children. You love them, you take care of them, but you know they aren't truly yours."

His mother's long sigh pulled Abdullah out of his memories. "Yumma, what Baba meant was to guard the key and pass it down to us. Insha'Allah, you'll live long enough to go back home, but you don't need to get yourself killed thinking you can return now. You've seen how those snipers shoot."

"I don't care if they shoot me. At least I'll die trying." She scanned his face again. "Why are you so pale?"

"Yumma, stop this, please. I don't need any more misery in my life. I want you to be content with what you have. Isn't that what you always tell me?" He enveloped his mom in a hug before adding, "And I was a little sick while you were away."

Her son's affection caused Um Abdullah to dissolve into tears. "I miss your father. He understood me best…"

Abdullah held his mother and let her cry. She'd feel better afterward. There was nothing he could say to soothe her. He missed his father, too. His grandfather—deeply. His little brother. His comrades, Omar and Ahmed.

Eventually, Um Abdullah pushed the blanket aside and wiped her eyes. "I'm making you some mint and sage tea. Don't go anywhere."

Chapter 40

Fatina: A Visit

AN AVALANCHE OF THOUGHTS flooded Fatina's mind. She felt caught in a tug-of-war, pulled in different directions. She cherished her small family and wanted them to be safe. She hoped her son would grow up strong and confident despite his amputation. But she didn't know how to help him—what to say, what to do, or how to guide him through a future she couldn't imagine.

Abdullah had urged her to visit Yumna and offer support. But how could she do that when she herself needed it most? Instead, she decided to visit a mother whose son was shot during the March and lost both of his legs. Making the decision took a lot of energy, but she needed to see how others dealt with similar challenges.

She knocked on Um Mahmoud's door, but it was already open. Many people left their doors unlocked during the day. The thought frightened Fatina because she imagined someone simply walking into the house. But in small, cramped neighborhoods like the Khan Younis refugee camp, where Um Mahmoud lived, everybody knew everybody, and no one could slip in unnoticed. Plus, with limited space in their homes, all the camp's kids played in the streets. So, they were used to this open-door lifestyle.

As she waited on the doorstep, she felt exposed in front of the men sitting outside their stores. "Go right in," one man said to her. "Um Mahmoud is inside." Fatina pushed open the door and stepped inside. She climbed the stairs, knocked on another open door, and called out, "Asalamu alaikum."

A kid came running. He stood staring at her as he bit into a sandwich, then called out, "Yumma, there's a woman for you." A woman hurried to the doorway. She wore a long, dark housedress and carried a small towel. She dried her hands as she greeted Fatina, "*Ahlan wa sahlan.*"

Fatina managed a smile as she returned the greeting. "*Ahlan feeki.* I'm Um Omar Mansour from the Amal neighborhood. I wanted to visit…" Fatina trailed off, offering Um Mahmoud a box of chocolates. "A small thing."

Um Mahmoud smiled and thanked her. The woman's features were soft but tired. She led Fatina to a small room with thin mattresses for seating, covered in dark brown, floral fabric. A heap of other mattresses and blankets was stacked at one end of the room, and a small, worn-out rug lay in the middle. Fatina removed her shoes and sat leaning against the wall. The woman handed her a cushion to place behind her back. "You're a reporter?" she asked.

"No," Fatina replied, understanding that Um Mahmoud was likely harassed by reporters, each wanting to hear her son's story, which didn't make her situation any easier.

"They come every day, and I tell them the same story. I'm sick of repeating it. I told my husband to talk to them."

"What about Mahmoud? Does he talk to the media?" Fatina asked.

The woman sat cross-legged, still clutching the towel as she spoke. She let out a short sigh but didn't answer the question. "Mahmoud was a soccer player. They shot him in both legs. We were all devastated at first, but my son is a very strong man."

As she continued, her tone shifted, gaining strength. "They thought they could crush us, but they haven't. I told my son, I said, 'Mahmoud, this isn't the end of life, habibi.' He even tried to go back to the March in his wheelchair, but I told him not to put me through more misery."

Fatina felt small. Um Mahmoud wasn't putting on an act. The honesty and passion with which she spoke were genuine. She was a mother who didn't try to hide her emotions, yet she also exuded strength. It was in the firmness of her voice, the resoluteness in her eyes, and the way she held her head up as she spoke of her son.

"I told Mahmoud that Allah is the Giver and He is the Taker. If He's taken both of your legs, He'll compensate you. You just need to be patient, I keep saying to him," she said, nodding as she finished.

Sitting silently, Fatina tried to hold back her emotions. But she struggled to swallow the lump in her throat, and a tear slid down her cheek. "*Mashallah*. I hope my son can be as strong as Mahmoud," she said, taking a deep breath.

"How old is your son?" Um Mahmoud asked.

"Seven."

"Habibi, may Allah protect him." She pressed her palm to her heart, then called out, "Maryam! Make us some tea."

Um Mahmoud continued speaking about her son and the day he was shot until a girl around fifteen came in. She set down a tray with two teacups, shook Fatina's hand, and smiled.

"This is Maryam. She's in ninth grade," Um Mahmoud said, admiring her daughter.

"She's beautiful. How many do you have?" Fatina knew the woman would be happy to talk about her kids. In Gaza, children were every woman's pride.

The woman's shoulders lifted subtly, and a satisfied grin appeared. "I have four boys and three girls. Two of the girls are married and have their own kids," she chuckled softly. "I'm a grandma now."

Fatina welcomed the change in mood as Um Mahmoud boasted about her children and grandchildren.

"They're my whole world. Insha'Allah, you'll become a grandmother. And when you do, believe me, you'll love your grandchildren more than anything. How many kids do you have?"

"I have Omar and Habiba," Fatina replied.

She instantly noticed Um Mahmoud's scrutiny, but she was used to it. People often asked her why she wasn't having more children. Fatina wanted to change the subject before it veered into babies and conception, but Um Mahmoud was quicker. "Insha'Allah, you'll have more. Have you tried?"

Fatina stammered a bit. "It's just how it is. Allah has given us two."

She silently hoped Um Mahmoud would stop there. She'd had some unpleasant encounters with nosy women prying into her reproductive life.

Once, while Fatina and Abdullah were waiting to see an obstetrician, the woman next to her turned and asked, "What are you here for?" Fatina, still young and unfamiliar with such intrusive ways, curtly replied, "Treatment." As soon as she responded, the woman was ready with her next question: "You have a problem, or your husband?" Fatina felt heat rise to her face at the audacity. She stayed silent, but that didn't deter the woman. "Your husband looks like a teacher." Fatina responded, "He isn't." Finally, she had had enough. Without a word, she stood and moved to Abdullah's other side, deliberately leaving a seat between herself and the woman.

Um Mahmoud was still talking. When she finished, Fatina asked, "Can I talk to Mahmoud?"

"Of course." Um Mahmoud called out for her daughter again, asking her to get Mahmoud.

After a few minutes, Mahmoud wheeled himself into the room. "Asalamu alaikum," he said.

Mahmoud was young and handsome, barely twenty. His light black hair was parted on one side, and he had the most beautiful smile. Although both of his legs were gone, it was heartening to see his smile remain.

"This is Um Omar Mansour. She wanted to see how you're getting along," Um Mahmoud said.

Fatina smiled and nodded. Um Mahmoud was courteous. She'd visit her again. For a moment, she didn't know what to say and feared she might get emotional. "*Alhamdulillah ala salamtak*, Mahmoud," she said—the safest prayer she could offer.

Mahmoud blushed as he lowered his gaze. "*Allahi salmik*, Khaltu."

Um Mahmoud's daughter served more tea and cookies as Mahmoud began talking about his passion for soccer. "Ball was my life. I was the team's goalkeeper, but we alternated, and I played on offense too. I still keep my soccer ball in my room and dribble with it. I'm looking forward to getting my prosthetics so I can play on the paraplegic team."

Fatina couldn't help but smile at Mahmoud's courage. He must have his bad moments, but she wouldn't dare meddle. "I admire your courage, Mahmoud," she said. "I hope my son can be like you in spirit. He lost his leg at the March."

"I'd be happy to meet him. We can play soccer together on the team."

Fatina thanked Mahmoud, and he left the room. Um Mahmoud swallowed hard before speaking. "You see how strong he appears? One night, I went into his room and found him crying his heart out. It's not as easy as it looks."

"It's not. But he could benefit from psychological support."

Fatina realized she had just echoed Abdullah's words. She'd never agreed to speak with a therapist about her injury and fears; opening up to a stranger was something she couldn't imagine. Instead, she occasionally got massages, which helped her relax in their own way.

"We had a therapist visit, but Mahmoud wasn't ready to talk to him," Um Mahmoud said. "I keep inviting his friends to come over. I don't want him to be cooped up in his room and die of a heart attack."

"Mahmoud is a very strong young man. His future will be bright, insha'Allah. He'll get married and have kids," Fatina said, trying to instill hope.

She thanked Um Mahmoud for spending time with her and promised to stay in touch. On her way home, Fatina reflected on several things. She'd finish Abdullah's portrait. She'd make sure Abdullah took Omar to the soccer team. As for therapy, she still wasn't convinced it would help her. She would gradually overcome her challenges. Maybe she could treat herself through art.

Chapter 41

Bilal: Love

THE COUPLE WAS TO SIGN the marriage deed at the Sharia court and then host a party at Dalia's house. But Dalia didn't want to see anyone, admitting she wasn't ready to socialize yet. Bilal was okay with that.

When he proposed to her, she broke down in tears. "You want to marry me?" she asked, barely getting the words out.

Bilal realized they were both profoundly hurt and unsettled. But it was the first time since Jasmine's death that he'd felt something good happening in his life, something he truly wanted. Dalia told him she was experiencing bouts of guilt, but she chose not to share details. He knew her story, but he wouldn't ask about it. Starting a new chapter would be the best thing for both of them.

To break the news to his mother, Bilal had taken Abdullah along—unable to face her interrogation alone. Abdullah understood him well. They sat in the living room while his mother carried in a tray of tea, cake, and nuts.

Abdullah spoke first. "Khaltu Um Bilal, I have good news about my friend Bilal," he began. "He's fallen in love."

Um Bilal tilted her head slightly, shifting her attention from Abdullah to Bilal and back again, trying to process what she'd just heard.

"It's true, Yumma," Bilal chimed in, his tone quietly pleading.

Um Bilal sat back, waiting for more. "*Allah yustur*. Go on."

They had agreed on a story they hoped would touch his mother. "This woman came into the store one day with her two boys," Abdullah continued. "The older one, about six, looked at Bilal and said to his mother, 'Mama, this man looks like Baba. But you say Baba is away…'"

Bilal liked the anecdote. Abdullah nodded at him, encouraging Bilal to take over. "Then I realized she lived near the store, so I asked around about her and the kids. She's divorced and lives with her mother," he said.

A crease formed between Um Bilal's brows. After a long pause, she asked, "So, you fell in love with this woman and her two children?"

"Yes," Bilal replied, facing his mother squarely.

Her facial features twisted and contorted as if she'd just been struck. "Bilal, this feeling of yours could be temporary. When you realize what you're getting yourself into, you might have second thoughts. Why would you want to be responsible for raising two kids who aren't yours?" Um Bilal questioned.

"Yumma, I didn't plan this, but it feels right. For Abdullah, it was love at first sight, too. Wasn't it, Abu Omar?" He turned to Abdullah.

Abdullah chuckled. "Yes."

"Seems like I'm the only one who didn't fall in love before I got married!" Um Bilal let out a dramatic sigh.

Bilal understood his mother's worries. What would people say? Her concerns always revolved around people's opinions.

"People don't need to know the details. Anyone who has a problem can come to me, and I'll take care of it," Bilal said flatly.

Sensing that things weren't going as well as they had hoped, Abdullah moved to their agreed-upon Plan B. He asked Bilal to make them some coffee. Bilal heard his friend say carefully, "Khaltu, I talked to Bilal a few weeks ago, and he wasn't so well."

Without missing a beat, Um Bilal asked, "What's wrong with him?"

"Nothing physical… he's still been tormented by what happened with Jasmine. He told me he'd never remarry and that he keeps having nightmares. So when he came to me with this, I made sure he knew what he was committing to and that it wasn't a whim. My brother-in-law, Hamza, married a widow with a son, and they're happy. I know Bilal. It can work for him, too. It's his choice," Abdullah finished calmly.

"I'm the one who's going to be harassed for this…" Um Bilal said, worry seeping into her voice.

"It's unfair to think of this woman, or any divorced woman, that way," Abdullah replied softly. "If she were my sister, I'd want her to be happy and remarry. Khaltu, there's nothing morally wrong with what Bilal is doing. And people won't dare poke their noses into his life. I know your son is someone who fights for what he believes in."

***

Bilal chose navy-blue pants and an off-white button-down shirt. His mother wanted him to wear a tuxedo, but he told her he'd feel overdressed. It was their first visit to Dalia's. They had signed the marriage deed at the Sharia court and agreed to skip any parties for now. The wedding would be a small family gathering. They hadn't yet set a date.

Dalia came in wearing a white silk maxi slip dress. She was dazzling. Bilal stood, took both her hands in his, and kissed them. It was their first intimate moment. He looked at her with quiet affection and said, "*Mabrook*." A rekindled tenderness filled his heart, bringing him a rare sense of peace. The lost child within him had finally found a home.

Dalia's fingers swept across her face. "I'm sorry," she said softly. "Tears of happiness."

She greeted Um Bilal with kisses on both cheeks and on her hand, as is customary among women in Gaza. Um Bilal and Um Masood went to another room, giving the couple privacy.

Bilal sat close to Dalia, their shoulders brushing. She shivered. "Are you cold?" he whispered, offering a comforting smile.

"Just a bit nervous…or excited." She caught Bilal's eye as her color slowly returned.

Bilal moved closer to her, their legs now touching. She cuddled against his shoulder and released a soft breath. "Take your time," Bilal said. "I know there are many things you might want—or not want—to say. But if you do, I'm here to listen."

"I'm so exhausted…" was all Dalia could say.

Bilal still wasn't eager to hear any of her old stories, and he was certain she wasn't keen to retell them. Sometimes, it's better to leave things unsaid until the right moment.

After their moment at Dalia's, they began spending more time together, finding comfort in each other's company. One day, Bilal suggested they go to the beach. He hoped the fresh air and views would cheer her up.

Resting lightly against him as they sat on the couch, Dalia's breath hitched. "I don't feel like seeing anyone…"

"Baby, listen. It's okay to let it out," he said, trying to encourage her. "You don't have to keep bottling up your feelings like this."

Her shoulders trembled as she cried, her words barely audible. "I can't…"

He let her cry as she clung to him. "I thought you were happy to be with me," he said softly.

"I am. Remember, if it weren't for you, I would've been dead."

Bilal knew Dalia would never forget who she had been related to or what she had gotten caught up in, but he wanted to help her heal from the guilt. "Tomorrow, I'm visiting families to deliver food baskets before

Ramadan. How about you come with me?" He hoped that involving Dalia in charitable work would help her feel worthy again.

"I'd love that," Dalia said, lifting her face. Tears had smudged her mascara, and Bilal gently blotted her cheeks. "I can't remember the last time I did anything g…" Her voice caught again, but she finished her thought, "But I want to do this."

The next day, Bilal picked up Dalia. They had a dozen baskets to distribute.

"You know all these families?" she asked.

"Yes, and all their details."

When they reached the first house, Dalia knocked while Bilal held the basket. A young girl appeared at the doorway. "Asalamu alaikum," Dalia beamed. Bilal felt at peace when he saw Dalia's energy and happiness as she spoke to the families and handed out gifts. They responded by showering them with prayers.

"You know what, habibi? I think I've found myself the best job in the world," Dalia said after they finished their rounds.

Bilal grinned, feeling triumphant. "We're going to the beach now. Remember, you promised?"

They walked down to the shore. Dalia slipped off her shoes. "You want to race?"

The horizon was like a painting. Vivid reds, oranges, and yellows streaked across the sky, announcing the approaching sunset. Bilal remembered how that same sinking sun once made him sad yet also comforted him, knowing it slipped beyond the horizon to shine elsewhere. Today, gloomy thoughts had vanished. He saw only hope, beauty, and love.

"I don't want to race," he said, instead picking Dalia up and twirling her until they both fell onto the sand. For the first time, he heard her peals of laughter and felt her come alive in his arms.

Chapter 42

Fatina: Final Touch

After visiting Um Mahmoud, Fatina's emotions were mixed. She admired Mahmoud's quiet bravery and optimism. But she knew that deep down, he was tormented by his loss.

He was such a handsome young man with a lively soul. She had a feeling he would start playing soccer again once he got his prosthetics. It was easy to imagine a good woman falling in love with him someday. He deserved someone who would help him feel whole again.

Somehow, Fatina felt that her own son would also be okay. He, too, would join the soccer team. He'd stop throwing fits about going out or seeing people. Whenever Abdullah wasn't around, and Fatina had to manage Omar alone, it crushed her spirit. But now she'd be more like Um Mahmoud. She'd hold Omar's gaze and tell him he was stronger than he thought. His disability wouldn't prevent him from living a full life.

These reflections lingered as she settled in front of the canvas. She still hadn't finished Abdullah's portrait. Assessing her work, she felt captivated by what she had painted so far. He stood with his arms crossed, his posture confident, and… the eyes. She needed to decide what she wanted them to convey and what expression he should wear.

With a fine-tip brush, Fatina began making delicate strokes. Abdullah had long eyelashes and almond-shaped jade-green eyes.

His words replayed in her mind as she painted: "I married an artist. Your art can heal you." He had said it so many times, but she was too stubborn to listen. She'd acted like her seven-year-old son—throwing tantrums and unable to accept that her hand was mangled for life. Abdullah gently pointed out that she still had her good hand, but she saw only what she had lost.

The portrait was ready. Contemplating it again, a quiet thrill of love and pride filled her. No matter what happened, Abdullah would remain her rock and her source of empowerment. She tried to push aside the causes of their recent arguments. They all boiled down to her paranoia about that other woman and her lack of self-confidence.

After her injury, Fatina often found herself studying other women's hands, hyper-aware of what she now lacked. Abdullah accepted her more than she accepted herself. Even when she was angry or upset, she'd remind herself that Abdullah was loving and had never once hurt her during their twelve years of marriage. She knew women who were abused, disrespected, or unloved, but she'd never experienced any of those things. The only form of torture that damaged her life was the occupation.

They had their fights, though, with Fatina dragging her pillow and blanket to the couch—something that always infuriated Abdullah. He'd shout, "If you're leaving this bed, then so am I!" and either sleep in the kids' room or leave the house altogether.

One evening, he stuffed his military gear into his backpack and muttered, "I'm on duty tonight." That was enough to bring Fatina back to her senses. Imagining something happening to him, she scolded herself. She even stood with her back to the door, like a child, and pleaded with him not to go. He finally dropped his bag and hugged her. "When you leave the room like that, you make the shaytan happy. Don't do that."

Admiring the portrait one more time, Fatina smiled. Then she turned it around and slid it into the corner of the room behind the curtains.

Chapter 43

Abdullah: A Journey

Um Abdullah wasn't the same after the last protest. Abdullah knew something was pulling her back to the fence. So he kept a close watch on her movements and made sure Khaltu Adla would never agree to take her again. When Um Abdullah returned to Quran lessons at the mosque, Abdullah worried she might be trying to persuade the other women to join the March.

His mother was doing laps around the kitchen table as he came in to check on her. "Asalamu alaikum," he said, kissing her on the forehead. "What are you up to, habibti?"

"Adla said I need to walk every day to make my legs stronger. Do you think they'll be good again?"

"I can take you to the gym if you like," he teased.

"You're making fun of me!" Um Abdullah shot him a pointed look, then resumed walking. "Laugh all you want. You won't catch me sitting down, being a useless old woman."

"I'm sorry, Yumma. I think it's a marvelous idea. Plus, you'll need to be in good shape if you want to go on a journey this Friday."

Um Abdullah paused, her breath short. She adjusted her hijab and looked at Abdullah. "You're taking me to the March?"

"No. Something better." His words carried a warmth that made her stand still. "How would you like to go pray at Al-Aqsa Mosque?"

Um Abdullah gasped. "*Ya Allah*! You better not be joking, or I'll spank you with my cane!"

Abdullah laughed and hugged his mother. "I'm serious, *wallah*. You and Khaltu Adla."

Um Abdullah was overwhelmed with excitement. She shouted with joy, "I need to call Adla!" and spun in circles, searching for her phone.

Abdullah scanned the room and spotted it on the sofa. He picked it up, dialed the number, and watched in amusement as his mother shared the good news with his aunt, her hand trembling as she held her phone. After she finished, she turned to her son. "Abdullah, you can't come with us?"

"Only men over 40 are given a permit, but women of any age can go," he said, knowing that even after he turned 40, it would still be hard for him to visit Al-Quds. Israeli soldiers guarded the crossing into occupied Palestine and could easily pick anyone out and imprison them.

"What about Fatina? Let her come along with us," Um Abdullah pleaded.

Abdullah couldn't explain things to his mother. He couldn't tell her he feared for Fatina's safety. Masood had definitely passed information about his involvement in the Resistance to Israeli intelligence. Even if they gave Fatina a permit, they could still interrogate and imprison her. He didn't dare tell Fatina, worried it would deepen her sense of entrapment, though he suspected she already understood. And what about his kids, who kept asking why they couldn't visit Al-Quds?

"Yumma, I need Fatina here with me. Maybe another time, insha'Allah."

"Abdullah, I have to get my bag ready, habibi." Um Abdullah left him standing, grinning with excitement.

Chapter 44

Alya: Al-Quds

AL-QUDS WAS ONLY 52 MILES from Gaza, but the trip took nearly six hours. First, all the travelers gathered at the Beit Hanoun Crossing in the northern Gaza Strip. The Israelis called it Erez. Alya and Adla sat in the waiting lounge.

"You're too excited! Get a grip," Adla said, laughing at her sister's beaming smile.

Alya's stomach fluttered with a mix of anxiety and excitement. She found it hard to believe she would be visiting another part of Palestine. For that part to be Al-Quds was every Palestinian's dream. Not many people were issued permits to visit.

The travelers had to walk down a long corridor leading to the Israeli checkpoint. Alya and Adla rode in a golf cart. They waited for two hours, and then Alya was called for interrogation. A female officer led her into a small room. She glanced back at Adla and nodded to reassure her.

Lowering herself into a plastic chair, she faced the male officer across the desk. "Good morning," he said, reading her name from the computer screen, "*Hajja* Alya."

Alya was praying silently, but her lips moved. She really wanted to say, "It'll be a good morning when I stop seeing your face," but she managed a brisk, "Good morning."

"Um Abdullah, why are you traveling to Jerusalem?" His eyes stayed on her as he swiveled his chair.

"To pray at Al-Aqsa."

"You have two sons and a daughter?"

"They were three; one was killed in a *qassef*." Alya clenched her jaw, restraining herself from adding, "by your cowardly planes."

"What does Abdullah do?"

Alya kept mumbling prayers to calm her nerves. She was a believer. Allah would grant her strength. She refused to let the officer intimidate her. "He's a teacher."

The soldier smirked and chuckled. "Um Abdullah, you're either naïve or trying to be difficult."

Abdullah had given her instructions on how to answer questions. He'd warned her that they might ask about people in the neighborhood—not because they knew everything, but because they wanted her to think they did. They would try to pressure her into talking, but most of it was just fishing for information. So, when the officer asked her about people in her neighborhood, she responded with general information. At one point, she told him she kept to herself and didn't socialize much.

"You went to the protests, Um Abdullah?" he asked.

"Yes, I did."

"Why?"

"Because I wanted to see my land." Alya didn't flinch.

"Your grandson got shot, and you nearly suffocated. The protesters are *mokharibin*. You should stay away from them."

Alya had been more polite in her answers than she expected, so she finally decided to risk saying what she felt without being reckless. "You've locked us up in a big cage. People are fed up."

"You know it's Hamas. They're the ones ruining your life there."

"All the Palestinian *shabab* are my children," she said calmly.

The interrogation continued for an hour. Her head began to ache from the tension, but she worried more about being turned back. Finally, the officer told her she could leave. Holding on to her cane, Alya pushed herself up from the chair.

When Adla saw her emerge from the interrogation room, she ran to her. Alya smiled proudly and said, "Come on, Adla. We're going to Al-Aqsa."

They rode in a small van with other people. Alya was like an enchanted child the entire ride, turning from one window to the other, drinking in every sight. The green-carpeted mountains. The abundant trees. The open skies.

"Look, Adla, how beautiful our country is..." Alya said, her face streaked with tears.

Adla wiped her own tears and put her arm around her sister. "Insha'Allah, we'll return one day."

Along the way, the driver pulled over at a spring gushing from a rock. They stepped out of the van and drank from it. Alya played with the water, splashing it on her cheeks. She stood with her hands on her hips, in awe of the lush hills surrounding them. She'd never felt so refreshed. If only time could stand still.

As they approached Al-Quds, Alya's heart fluttered. Adla asked her about the interrogation, but Alya was too entranced to go into details. "Who cares about them? They're pathetic. They thought they could get me to work with them."

Adla laughed. "Because they saw how smart you are."

They were entering a road that led to Al-Aqsa. Amid the stone walls and wide gates of the timeless Old City, Alya felt as if she had been transported to another time. The entire atmosphere evoked a strong sense of nostalgia. She was at home, but in a house that had been stolen from her. Her fury at seeing Israeli soldiers walking freely in the area turned into choking tears.

The Dome of the Rock was a masterpiece of architecture. With its flawless Quranic inscriptions beneath the Dome, intricate mosaics, and marble, it was perfection. Alya and Adla stepped inside to pray. As she pressed her feet into the red carpet, Alya felt as if the mosque were giving her a big hug. A glow of serenity enveloped her. She prayed in every corner and sat, contemplating the architecture and the way people kept coming despite daily harassment by Israeli settlers and police.

***

After nearly two days in Al-Quds, a new energy coursed through Alya's body. Adla noticed her sister's gait was more energetic. "You're a new human being! Look at your steps. They're confident and powerful, *mashallah*," she said.

Alya remained lively throughout her time in Al-Quds. She imagined living there and how it would give her life new meaning. "My soul returned to me once I saw Al-Aqsa Mosque. I feel young again," she boasted, her face beaming.

When she'd gone on pilgrimage to Mecca, Alya had become emotional and her soul had soared, but this was different. This was a holy mosque on her land. She was adamant that it would one day return to its rightful owners. She pictured Amer smiling before her. "I know you're happy for me, habibi," she said.

Before their visit ended, the sisters couldn't pass up the opportunity to pray Fajr at Al-Aqsa. As they sat on the carpet after prayer, Alya heard a commotion outside. Voices were chanting, "Allahu Akbar!" A few women around her recited the Quran, paying no heed. She called out to one, "Sister, what is the noise outside?"

The woman calmly finished reciting a verse, then looked in Alya's direction and said, "Soldiers trying to barge into the mosque, as usual."

Alya's eyes widened. "And what do you do?"

"Wait and see, sister," the woman said listlessly, as if the matter were too trivial to interrupt her recitation of the Quran.

A moment later, the sound of boots clomping and gear rustling grew louder. Men and women rushed to the gate to prevent the soldiers from storming in, but the soldiers shoved them with batons and rifle butts. The scene quickly descended into mayhem. The people inside the mosque tried to fend off the soldiers with chairs and whatever they could lay their hands on. Some threw shoes at them. An explosive sound rocked the mosque.

Alya, Adla, and another woman ducked behind a stone column. An elderly man reading the Quran tumbled as a soldier pushed the wooden stand he had been gripping for support. Someone helped him to his feet, and he hobbled slowly to a wall.

The March in Gaza had been one thing, but this—so close, so personal—was unlike anything she had experienced.

Alya's eyes burned, and her throat was on fire. Tear gas again! Adla pulled her hand as they tried to escape through another gate. "There's no other exit!" a woman shouted. The Israelis allowed them to use only two of the mosque's gates, and both were blocked.

Smoke and the sound of shattering glass filled the mosque. It was hard to make out what was happening. The woman standing nearby sprayed a solution onto Alya and Adla's hijabs and instructed them to cover their faces until the chaos ended.

"How long does this usually last?" Adla shouted to the woman.

"They wreak havoc and detain a few men, and that satisfies them for the day."

"*Allah yakhudhum*," Alya cursed, adding a prayer for safety. It was clear that Al-Quds had its share of Israeli terror every day.

The woman was right. Alya peeked from behind the column and saw soldiers yanking kneeling young men to their feet. The mosque had been turned into a battlefield, and the carpet was littered with broken glass, tear gas canisters, and rocks. A thick gray dust settled on it.

Somehow, Alya wasn't terrified. She drew strength from the people around her, awed by how the worshipers remained unshaken amid the attacks.

With each explosion, Alya ducked. The soldiers threw stun grenades into the mosque. The shock made her legs shake and her arthritic hands tremble, causing her to lose her grip on her cane. A soldier approached Alya, Adla, and the two women, shouting orders in Hebrew for them to evacuate. Alya gripped her sister's arm for support.

As they made their way across the mosque, they saw three soldiers attacking a young man with their rifle butts. Alya stopped, raised her hand in protest, and shouted, "Let him go!" She started towards the soldiers, but Adla pulled her back.

A woman walked straight to the soldiers huddled around the man and broke through the circle. She shielded the man's body with her own, and Alya heard her scream, "Allahu Akbar! Leave him alone."

When she reappeared, her hijab was splattered with blood.

Once the chaos subsided, men, women, and even children grabbed brooms and started cleaning up the mess. Alya loved their shared sense of responsibility. "Adla, let's clean up with them," she said. "I want to feel like I've done something for the mosque."

Alya noticed that the people of Al-Quds had just resumed their lives as if nothing had happened. Not that anyone could grow used to such terror, but they had learned to hold their ground against the soldiers who invaded and desecrated their mosque—and to cope with the aftermath.

The permit Alya and Adla received allowed them to visit Al-Quds only, so they decided to spend part of the morning touring the Old City. Every time they stopped at a mosque, a shop, a monument, or even a wall, Alya posed and asked Adla to take pictures, her smile wide and full of life. "You look gorgeous in all the pictures, Alya," Adla repeated with each photo she snapped.

They shopped at Souk Bab Al-Amood, and Alya bought little treasures for her children and their families: jewelry for the women and girls, T-shirts for the men and boys, and Al-Aqsa souvenirs for everyone as a token of their connection to the holy site. She stopped at a spice merchant who had heaps of spices displayed in huge bags. "Give me 250 grams of allspice, sumac, and turmeric, and half a kilo of za'atar," Alya said to the man.

"But we have all this in Gaza, *yakhti*," Adla said.

"But these are from Al-Quds," Alya reasoned. "They carry the aroma of Palestine."

Chapter 45

Alya: A Reunion

Two days weren't enough to satisfy Alya's longing. She wanted to see other parts of Palestine. Of course, it would be impossible, as it was rare for anyone from Gaza to be granted a permit to enter occupied Palestinian cities like Yafa, Haifa, Lidd, and Akka. But she thought she might be able to see her sister-in-law, who lived in Bethlehem, and that would be better than nothing.

"Adla, let's call Siham to see if we can visit her," she suggested.

Adla, sitting on a step in the souk, was drained from all the activity and long walks. "Alya, do you know what that means? We'd have to go through the Tarqumiya military checkpoint. That's like passing through hell."

Alya frowned, feeling the strain on her already creased forehead. "I really want to see Siham. I'd feel like I was seeing Amer, *Allah yirhamu.*"

They hailed a taxi to the infamous Tarqumiya checkpoint. It took two hours to reach it. The sisters grabbed their bags and got out of the cab. With all the shopping Alya had done, they had to carry three bags: two on wheels and one over Adla's shoulder.

Alya gawked at the grim spectacle. A long cage had appeared before them. She couldn't see the end of it; it was packed with people, herded like sheep. "Is there an end to this line, Adla?"

Adla pulled a prayer rug from her bag, spread it on the ground, and sat down. "Looks like we're stuck, Alya. Come sit."

Three hours passed. They eventually had to stand in line, but Alya sat on the ground when her legs could no longer support her. They inched forward, the line hardly moving.

Adla asked the man in front of her, "Do they let everyone in before dark?"

The man leaned against the cage. "Yes, if we behave. Tomorrow morning, I'll go through this again," he said, lighting what must have been his sixth cigarette since they got in line.

After finally getting through the cage, they reached the revolving gates. They were automatic, so if someone didn't push fast enough, the bars would slam into them. Adla was swift enough to pass, but Alya didn't make it through. Her hijab slipped off and got caught in the bars. She began screaming, but the soldiers remained on the other side, snickering. People couldn't speak up, or they'd be forced to wait endlessly.

When Alya made it out, she collapsed onto the ground, panting. Adla helped her up and whispered in her ear, "Don't curse or say anything. Let's go."

Siham was waiting on the other side, but Alya could hardly focus. She clutched her cane with trembling hands as pins and needles shot up her legs. Her sister-in-law recognized Alya and waved. Alya laughed as she threw herself into Siham's arms and cried, "You're as beautiful as ever, Siham!"

In her early sixties, Siham was Amer's youngest sister. Her face was round and full, her cheeks glowing red. "So are you, Alya!"

All three hugged, kissed, and cried—Alya more from exhaustion.

"Don't tell me you have to pass through this hell gate every day, Siham," Alya said.

Siham held Alya's hand and guided her to a taxi. "Ah, Um Abdullah, where do I begin? My sons do; may Allah be with them. Let's go home so you can rest."

In the car, Alya saw the separation wall. It snaked around Bethlehem, giving the city a siege-like appearance. "I didn't know the wall was so tall. It literally cages you in," Adla said.

Siham sighed. "It separates us from our olive grove and from Al-Quds."

Alya studied the wall. Revolutionary artwork covered every inch, protesting the occupation, the injustice, and the wall itself. Emptiness gripped her. A lump rose in her throat, and her chest tightened.

"See this picture? A famous *ajnabi* artist painted it," Siham said.

"Slow down, *yakho*," Alya told the driver so she could take a good look. It was a dove holding a tiny olive branch in its beak, its chest in the crosshairs of a weapon. She exhaled. "*La ilaha illa Allah.*"

Everything felt dreary. Still, the city was beautiful. It had the aura of holy places. Ancient buildings made of royal stone gave it a sense of timelessness. "These are just like the stones at Al-Aqsa, see, Adla?"

"Yes. Bethlehem was part of Al-Quds once upon a time. But now it's divided by this ugly wall," Siham said.

They arrived at The Walled Off Hotel. "An odd place to build a hotel," Adla said.

"It belongs to that *ajnabi* artist," Siham said.

As they entered the Dheisheh refugee camp, where Siham lived, the view grew bleaker. Houses, crammed together, suffocated the narrow streets. Alya thought about how refugee camps were all the same—some just more dilapidated than others. "If I didn't know where I was, I would've thought I was at Khan Younis Camp in Gaza," Alya commented.

"*Ahlan wa sahlan,*" Siham said as the driver pulled over.

Leading them into her kitchen, Siham proudly announced, "I've made you *msakhan* with olive oil from our trees." She soaked the saj bread in broth and olive oil, then spread it on a platter and topped it with cooked onions.

"Amer used to tell me that your cooking was the best. I was never jealous," Alya laughed.

"So you got to harvest your trees this season?" Adla asked.

"We managed to salvage a few of them. The rest, they burned. The settlers barge onto our land like mad dogs every season."

Alya hadn't expected to feel so depressed by the visit. What she had envisioned as an enjoyable detour was taking a heavy toll on her. Bethlehem was just another Palestinian city under occupation. Inside the city, people moved about freely. But right across from the entrance stood an Israeli military station.

"I don't understand," Adla said. "If Bethlehem is under the Palestinian Authority, why is there an Israeli military presence across from the gate?"

"To show who's really in charge," said Siham. "The Palestinian Authority has no authority over anything on the ground."

"Your situation is more messed up than ours in Gaza," Adla observed.

Alya dug into the *msakhan*. Smacking her lips, she savored the lemony taste of the sumac and the olive oil-drenched bread. "You still make it the same way, Siham, habibti. Your hands are blessed."

This was Amer's favorite dish. When Alya made it, she would boast that every ingredient was local—even the chicken was raised at home. She made the saj bread herself, and most importantly, the olive oil came from their land.

She imagined what it must be like for Siham and others to have fanatic Israeli settler mobs burn their trees. It made her stomach drop, but she tried to push the images away so she could enjoy the rest of her meal.

Despite it all, a gentle, resilient smile lingered on Siham's lips. "I know it's horrible what those settlers do, but you know, I pray for my trees the same way I pray for my children. And Allah blesses me every year."

"I'm glad you can maintain your faith and high spirits," Adla said.

***

The trip back to Gaza wasn't as arduous. Alya clung to memories of Al-Quds and tried to forget Bethlehem. Al-Aqsa Mosque was etched into her memory. She'd absorbed every detail—even the stone floor outside. Remembering how lucky she'd been to visit Al-Quds, she felt so invigorated and uplifted that she almost smiled at the soldiers.

When they reached the Beit Hanoun Crossing, Abdullah and the kids were waiting for them.

Um Abdullah called out, "Abdullah!" and waved vigorously. Habiba ran to her as Abdullah helped Omar with his new prosthetic. "Did you miss me already?" Alya asked as Habiba hugged her. The little girl was nearly the same height as her grandmother.

"Tata, did you take photos?" Habiba's eyes gleamed with excitement.

"Of course, habibti. My phone has dozens of pictures. Dozens."

When Abdullah approached his mother, she clung to him and cried out of happiness. Then she faced Omar and enveloped him in a long, protective hug, whispering, "Habibi, I missed you." Turning back to Abdullah, she grabbed his arm and said, "Those bastards couldn't get to me."

"You look like you drank from the fountain of youth, Um Abdullah!" Abdullah teased, wrapping his arm around his mother's shoulders.

"Alya was like a curious child the whole time. You should've seen how she walked around and insisted on exploring everything," Adla said.

Um Abdullah leaned on her son as they walked to the car. "You know, Abdullah, habibi, I feel like this journey has given me a new lease on life. Imagine what would become of me if I went back to our home in Al-Majdal."

"Insha'Allah, we'll return, Yumma."

Stopping mid-stride, she said, "Abdullah, we were attacked inside the mosque. Exactly like we see in those videos."

"Seriously?"

"But we weren't scared of those cowards. Nobody in there was." She held up her index finger as if giving a sermon.

"Did you see settlers?" Abdullah asked.

"No, alhamdulillah. The people told us the settlers sometimes come in the morning. They provoke worshipers inside the mosque by invading the vicinity, and the soldiers just stand by and let them do as they wish. *Allah yakhudhum!*" Um Abdullah huffed as she got into the car.

"Let's go home," Abdullah said, happily. "Fatina made your favorite dish."

Chapter 46

Abdullah: Home

Back at home, everyone gathered around Um Abdullah. With her invigorated voice and lively demeanor, Abdullah thought his mother looked as though she had just liberated Al-Quds from occupation. "I should've sent you there a long time ago," he said.

"I'm going again, insha'Allah, insha'Allah!" Um Abdullah interjected.

Habiba scrolled through the photos on her grandmother's phone as Omar leaned in beside her. "Here's a soldier!" Omar shouted, pointing at the screen. "Tata, did the soldiers shoot people?"

"They shot into the air to scare us," Um Abdullah replied.

She leaned closer to Abdullah and lowered her voice. "They asked me lots of questions about you. I told them, 'You think my son tells me when or where he comes and goes? Plus, I don't have time for him. I take Quran lessons and have my own life.'" She laughed at her own wit.

Abdullah was proud of his mother and reassured by how little she knew about his work in the Resistance. He never told her much because he believed that, in this situation, ignorance was best. "That's my mother!" he kissed her head.

While he felt relieved, the questions the Israelis asked his mother confirmed his suspicions: they knew something about him. Now

Abdullah was sure he'd never be able to visit Al-Quds, at least as long as it remained under occupation.

He'd seen men take the risk of traveling through the crossing only to be captured, imprisoned, and sentenced to years in prison. One had worked as an aid worker with an international humanitarian organization in Gaza. When he tried to pass through Beit Hanoun, he was arrested and accused of funding terrorist organizations. The claims were baseless, yet that didn't stop them from sentencing him to twelve years. By all accounts, going through the Beit Hanoun Crossing was a gamble.

While the others talked, Fatina set the table and called out that dinner was ready.

"You made *maftool* yourself, Fatina?" Alya exclaimed, astonished.

"You doubt my culinary prowess, Khaltu?" Fatina asked, laughing.

"But I mean… you made it from scratch?"

Abdullah and Fatina exchanged a glance, and Abdullah said, "You know we can't make *maftool* like you, Yumma."

After dinner, Fatina whispered to Abdullah that she had a surprise for him upstairs. Her face glowed, and peace washed over him—something he hadn't felt with Fatina in a while.

"Close your eyes," she said, then turned the easel to reveal the portrait. "Now."

Abdullah opened his eyes to see his own portrait. In it, he stood tall, arms crossed, his eyes holding an unexpected warmth beneath their firm resolve. At the top, Fatina had painted the words "My Hero" in bold strokes.

He couldn't help but tear up. Walking over to Fatina, Abdullah gently drew her into a warm embrace. It had been a long time since he had last cried. Pushing his feelings aside had taken a heavy toll on Abdullah. Fatina's response to the abduction—and everything that followed—only worsened the situation.

When his comrade Omar was alive, Abdullah would open up to him. They lived under the same circumstances, and he was the one who understood him best. During breaks on duty, they'd spend long nights sitting under a tree, talking about the present and the future. After Omar was martyred, Abdullah struggled to find anyone who truly got him the way Omar did.

In fact, he became the one who took care of his comrades. Assuming a leadership role entailed sacrifices, pent-up emotions, unspoken words, and a weight he often carried alone. Fatina chastised him for it, and they argued frequently. She saw through him, but he pretended everything was under control. Writing became his personal therapy, a way to speak his mind at last.

Fatina wept in his arms. "I'm back to my art, just like you always wanted."

Abdullah kissed her tears away, and she wiped his with her thumbs. "Your work is going to be famous," he said.

"I just want to be… well…" Fatina sobbed.

Abdullah lovingly stroked her hair. "You're healthy, you're beautiful, and you're okay. If you ask Allah for strength, He will empower you. Trust me. And we can always talk."

Fatina's crying subsided. "You approve of me becoming famous and having my pictures all over the internet?" she asked, a smile tugging at her lips.

"I'll be the acclaimed artist's husband."

Chapter 47

Abdullah: A New Phase

ABDULLAH RECEIVED A CALL from Othman. They hadn't spoken since Abdullah had quit the club.

"There's been a development with the Great March of Return. If you'd like, come to the meeting," Othman said.

Since Omar's shooting and amputation, Abdullah had lost touch with the protests. He had become consumed with responsibilities, stumbling through a new reality in which he had to care for his amputee son—something he had never been prepared for. Even his military training seemed useless in helping him handle Omar. He considered Othman's invitation but couldn't decide what he really wanted. Did he have the energy to go back to the protests, if that's where Othman was going with this?

"I don't know, Othman. My life's been a bit tangled up lately," he replied.

"How about we meet up, the two of us, and talk further?" Othman countered.

"*Mashi.* Let me know when and where."

Othman suggested a restaurant, but Abdullah preferred the open air. Enclosed spaces made him feel claustrophobic. He noticed this change in himself after the kidnapping. In many ways, it mirrored his feelings of confinement under the siege. The beach was the only place that offered a horizon and let him breathe without feeling constrained.

True, it wasn't an entirely free beach. It was accessible only for a few miles out into the sea, but for the sake of his mental health, he liked to believe otherwise. He'd even formed a bond with the sea and its waves, rising high, falling, and constantly rising again. The sea had become his empowering ally.

It was 3 p.m. when Abdullah met Othman at a roadside spot facing the beach, where access to cheap wooden tables and chairs cost just five shekels. The place sold coffee and herbal tea. Abdullah ordered coffee.

As they shook hands and sat down, Abdullah quickly assessed Othman. He wore a puzzled, or rather curious, expression. It was obvious he'd be asking questions.

Othman traced the rim of his coffee cup, then said, "You've been away for a while. I hope everything is okay."

Abdullah sipped his coffee. It was bitter, but its heat comforted him. "Busy with family issues. My son and the prosthetic. It's not easy."

"May Allah help you," Othman offered sincerely.

A sudden headache hit Abdullah. He leaned on the table, pressing his temples. That's how it had been since the incident; the headaches would strike without warning. They'd either fade after a few minutes or linger for the rest of the day. He reached into his jacket to fish out a painkiller.

"Are you all right?" Othman asked.

"Been getting these migraine attacks lately."

The doctor had told him to cut back on coffee. The nausea also made coffee both repulsive and tasteless. He pushed the cup aside, opened a bottle of water, and swallowed two Panadols.

"I met with the Great March of Return organizing committee this week. They're planning a new phase," Othman said.

Abdullah tried to stay engaged. Just over a month had passed since the March began, and already more than forty-five had been killed, not to mention the amputees and injured. He wasn't sure the protest was leading anywhere. Not that he undervalued its purpose, but the people were paying a heavy price.

"I think the March is a great example of popular resistance, but there's only so much we can do," Abdullah said. "If we continue, I only see more people getting killed. And the world doesn't see our dead, or us."

"They want to cross the separation fence," Othman said. "They suggested we have the protestors hold hands and march toward it."

Abdullah sat in silence for a moment, deep in thought. The idea seemed fanciful to him. "Are we getting any kind of international support for this? Who will stand behind us?" he asked rhetorically.

Othman snorted. "International support? The only thing foreigners are interested in at the March is taking pictures of people dancing dabke and children holding up flags. They keep saying, 'We have to show the humanity of the Palestinians.' I can't stand how they water down the March to 'human stories.' The March itself is a human story! We are human." He puffed and gulped down the rest of his coffee.

Abdullah nodded. "I know what you mean. I often hear writers and journalists say we have to appeal to internationals by showing the human side of our struggle. You know, Othman..."

He leaned back and crossed his arms. His head throbbed, and he knew he wouldn't be able to keep the conversation going much longer.

"The very first protest on March 30… you know what I felt? Seeing hundreds of people gathered behind the fence, protesting this military siege and demanding the right to return to our land, made me realize how literally caged in we are. Although we stood in the open air, the claustrophobia I felt was overwhelming. As for the committee's idea, we won't know until we try. But we must be aware that it may well prove catastrophic."

Othman nodded. "So, you're saying we'll be on our own… as usual?"

"That goes without saying. We could work on creating an atmosphere and building momentum. But then again, we're not selling products."

"So maybe you can come to the meeting…" Othman tried.

"I can't commit to meetings these days, but I'll be where you can find me." A high-pitched ringing filled Abdullah's ears. "I need to go…"

"What's that scar on your neck, Abdullah?"

Abdullah was taken aback. He scanned the table as if searching for the answer. He could feel Othman examining him. "I had an accident," he said, avoiding his colleague's gaze.

In Othman's tone, Abdullah heard many unspoken words. He thought Othman was a decent guy, but he needed to maintain a level of formality.

"Abdullah, I admire your professionalism and discretion. I think those are two things we have in common." Othman grinned, intertwining his fingers and twiddling his thumbs. He lowered his voice and glanced sideways before continuing, "I've never told you this, but I've worked with a documentary filmmaker on the Resistance."

The café overlooked the beach, but Abdullah could feel the air growing still. He weighed what he'd just heard. Was Othman that kind of person? "The Resistance?" Abdullah prodded.

"I collaborate with the Doha Channel on documentaries about the Resistance. When I read your story about the balaclava men, I thought it was brilliant. That's when I realized our interests intersect. If you'd like to be part of the work I'm doing, I think it would be a golden opportunity for both of us." Othman finished his proposal and picked up his keys.

When Abdullah decided to join the writers' club, he asked around about Othman and the others. But no one told him that the guy was working for the Resistance. He hadn't underestimated him; Othman simply seemed more scholarly. Now he realized how wrong he had been. Abdullah knew that truly intelligent people believed in the power and legitimacy of the Resistance. He recalled a famous martyr, Basil Al-Araj, known for being both an intellectual and a freedom fighter.

They got up, Abdullah pressing his forehead with one hand. He needed to go home and think through everything they'd discussed—which would likely make his headache worse.

Chapter 48

Abdullah: Back to Work

That evening, Abdullah's regiment had a meeting. The painkillers had eased the pain, and the headache had subsided somewhat. He'd been on sick leave. The doctor had diagnosed him with post-concussion syndrome. The commanding officer, Oday, told him he'd give him a month to recuperate. But Abdullah missed his comrades and wanted to attend the meeting, if only to see them. He wasn't sure how Oday would react.

It was a warm, sticky, almost mid-May evening, one of the first truly hot spells leading into summer. Inside the city, the air felt trapped among the crowded concrete structures. But as soon as Abdullah reached more open areas, he felt a light wind. It was far from refreshing, but at least the stifling feel of the city had disappeared.

When he arrived at the military base, the guard identified him, opened the gate, and greeted him warmly. "Abood, welcome back!" They shook hands.

"Where's Oday?" Abdullah asked.

The man pointed left. "His office."

His comrades would be surprised, and Abdullah hoped Oday would be happy to see him after his absence. The military base housed an administrative office at the far left end, with the rest of the space used for training. Abdullah knocked on the office door and walked in. "Asalamu alaikum."

An uproar erupted as everyone called out, "Abdullah!" in unison. They stood to greet him, bumping fists and hugging.

He told Oday that his concussion hadn't worsened, that he wanted to return early, and that he could perform some duties. "Your doctor said you needed rest, Abdullah. I don't want to see you get hurt on duty," Oday said.

"I've been through worse," Abdullah replied, recalling the time he fell ill after Ahmed died in the tunnel. He'd developed a high fever and spent two weeks sleeping, barely aware of what was happening around him.

Oday agreed to let him return, but restricted him to half-day shifts, no nights.

The following day, Abdullah reported for watch duty east of Khan Younis. Days weren't as magnificent as nights, but there was always something profound about watch duty. Standing there, Abdullah felt the enormity of his responsibility and that of his comrades.

They were the city's protectors against Israeli incursions. They were the ones who stayed alert to ensure people could go about their daily lives. They were an army, an honorable one, even if the world insisted on calling them terrorists. They were born under occupation and grew up within the struggle.

Through his binoculars, Abdullah could see the Israeli soldiers stationed behind the fence. He imagined the March committee's plan in action: people holding hands as they approached the fence. There would be no chance. What would stop the snipers from shooting?

May 14 was set as the day to breach the fence. People across the Gaza Strip would gather for the protest. First, a committee member would give a speech, and then they would proceed with the plan. Abdullah knew his people were fearless and would have no second thoughts about carrying this out. Would Fatina agree to be part of it? He couldn't preach this to others while worrying about protecting his own family.

He was grateful she'd picked up her paintbrushes again. Perhaps it was a sign of healing. The March and what might happen there could not only undo her progress but also have even more detrimental effects.

Abdullah went back to observing. The Israeli snipers were all in heavy gear, holding high-tech weapons generously supplied by their allies. He thought about how, during every military attack, they tested new weapons on the Palestinians. Once it was dense-metal explosives, then white phosphorus, and now F-35 fighter jets. His son had been shot with a butterfly bullet that exploded on impact, pulverizing tissue, arteries, and bone.

Despite being part of the Resistance for years, Abdullah still marveled at how disciplined his fellow freedom fighters were. They saw the snipers up close yet still resisted the urge to shoot. It wasn't fair that they had to constantly hold back while Israeli soldiers killed at will. But then again, living under occupation was the epitome of injustice.

During his break, Abdullah sat with his comrades under a formidable, ancient oak tree that gave him a sense of safety. Something was soothing about feeling the soil beneath him and the branches overhead, which shielded them from the sun. All four ate the rice-and-chicken dish *qidra*.

"I can't imagine anything that could taste better than Palestinian food," Ali said, chewing.

"That's because you've never been outside Gaza to taste anything else," Adel replied.

Abdullah dug into the moist, spiced rice platter. "My mother needs to hear this. She'd go on about all her homemade dishes."

The tree's shade made the hot weather bearable. A drone buzzing above provided part of life's daily soundtrack.

Even after everything he had faced recently, Abdullah felt at peace. He found calm in the camaraderie, the noble path of resisting occupation, and the determination to seek freedom. Yet there was also a gut-wrenching restlessness amid the constant, lifelong battle they were forced to wage.

As always, the weight of that generational struggle made his thoughts drift to his father and grandfather. Their stories had also shaped Abdullah's affinity for the land and his understanding of what had been lost—and what they were fighting for.

"Everybody in Al-Majdal owned land," his grandfather would say proudly. "Everybody wore the same clothing. The women wove fabric and made *thobes*. The nearby villages cultivated land and fished at sea. Everybody worked at what they were good at."

"And what did you do, Siddo?" Abdullah asked him. He could still see himself as a child, repeating the same question again and again. He liked asking it, knowing his grandfather's face would light up every time.

"Ask your grandmother; she'll tell you how I took care of the land. She envied those trees and said to me, 'You love those trees more than me.'" He'd laugh. "What did I do? In the evenings, I sat in my copper shop so she wouldn't be jealous of the trees anymore."

Their home still held remnants of his grandfather's copperware. Now, covered in a green, moldy patina, the pieces stood as a testament to neglect.

"Do you guys think that if people reached the frontier, they could get over the fence and cross into their lands?" Abdullah threw the question at his comrades, and the men answered between mouthfuls.

"They'll be shot instantly," Ali said flatly.

"Another massacre, and no one would care," Adel added.

"Sure, people will protest the killings. But at the highest level, world leaders will just express concern about our situation," Ali said, setting down his spoon and adjusting his legs. "The world only understands the language of power, not the language of sissies. The demonstrations have proved fatal, though they've been peaceful. I say we bomb the hell out of those bastards."

Abdullah wanted to believe that the March would be the way to return to their cities and lands, but the reality was too obvious and distressing.

Oday joined the men and made an unexpected announcement. "There's going to be a military maneuver tomorrow."

"What's the occasion?" Abdullah asked.

"We got word that the March is escalating. The protesters plan to get closer to the fence and try to cross over," Oday said, running a hand over his beard the way he did when something didn't sit right with him. It was apparent he was skeptical, too.

"We were just discussing possible scenarios if that happens," Abdullah said.

"There's only one scenario, and everyone knows it. And when it gets bloody, we might retaliate, and Allah knows what would happen after that," Oday said, then left.

Chapter 49

Fatina: Some Courage

"What's the matter, Abood?" Fatina snuggled up beside Abdullah on their bed. He lay on his back, an arm over his eyes.

"I can't take part in the maneuver," he answered.

"You'll be back when you feel better," she said, rubbing his arm. "Why is there a maneuver?"

"Just a procedure…"

"I'd like to watch a military maneuver. You think it might make my heart stronger, Aboodi?"

"You're already a braveheart," Abdullah said, stroking Fatina's hair.

"Abood, I wish you would teach me to use a weapon—a small gun that fits comfortably in my hand. Hamza taught Ayah; he took her somewhere, and they practiced."

Abdullah tilted Fatina's chin up. "You want to learn how to shoot? You weren't made for such things, baby." He smiled.

"Abood, I feel ignorant. Everyone needs to know how to defend themselves," she said, her composure faltering as a tear fell onto Abdullah's arm. "But with this hand, I can't."

Deep down, Fatina wasn't fixated on using a weapon. She never pictured herself shooting, even for sport. But she thought that maybe having marksmanship skills would help her build up her courage.

"I thought you might want to stick with horseback riding. You're improving at it," Abdullah said.

"I love horseback riding, but I want to be more versatile. I want to be the artist who holds a brush in one hand and a weapon in the other." She giggled.

"You've come a long way, love." Abdullah kissed her forehead. "There's no reason we can't try, but you need to get in shape first."

***

Fatina still didn't have the heart to go back to the March. Every time she thought of the fence, images of the shooting, the screams, and the blood overwhelmed her. But she reminded herself that even mothers of martyrs returned to the March, so why couldn't she?

Monday arrived. Unlike the usual Friday protest, May 14 was a special demonstration timed to coincide with the ceremony marking the relocation of the U.S. embassy to Al-Quds. Abdullah's mother insisted on attending, but he bribed her to stay home. "If anything happens, Allah forbid, you won't be able to go to Al-Quds again," he had told her.

The doorbell rang, and Fatina answered the intercom. "Who is it?"

"It's Um Mahmoud. You want to go to the March together?" Fatina couldn't respond. "Um Omar?" she heard her visitor ask.

"Yes, come on up, Um Mahmoud." She buzzed her in.

Fatina greeted Um Mahmoud, and they sat together in the guest room. She was radiant in her *thobe*. "Did you stitch this yourself? It's lovely," Fatina said, admiring the red embroidery, accented with other hues.

Um Mahmoud patted her dress. "My mother made it for me when I got married. You know it has to be in every bride's wardrobe. But I'm afraid I couldn't do the same for my daughter when she got married. I had someone else stitch hers."

"Was it as beautiful as yours?" Fatina didn't know why she'd steered the conversation to embroidery.

"No. My mother-in-law wasn't pleased. She said I needed to make it at home to preserve the tradition. I told her I'd need a new pair of eyes." Um Mahmoud laughed.

A hush fell between them, and Fatina's shoulders slumped as she tried to think of what to say.

"I know it's hard, but today will be different," Um Mahmoud said, clearly sensing Fatina's apprehension. "Everybody will hold hands to form a long human chain. Then we'll approach the fence and demand to cross into our lands. That's what they said." She grinned, her excitement palpable.

Fatina admired the lady's enthusiasm. What had happened to her son hadn't extinguished her spark. Her fearlessness and determination were genuine.

"I'm not sure I can…" Fatina trailed off.

"If your husband told you not to go, then…" Um Mahmoud hesitated.

"No, Abdullah didn't even bring up the subject."

They sat for a while, chatting over tea and cookies. Finally, Fatina decided she could go, and maybe just avoid venturing near the fence.

She got up, put on a black embroidered abaya, and elegantly wrapped her head in a keffiyeh. Maybe this was what she needed: to face her fears. Yes, she'd break the barrier and go. All those women couldn't be braver than her. She was made of the same Palestinian soil, with the same strength coursing through her. She'd raise the flag high and chant with her people.

"I'm ready," she said, her eyes shining as she waved her flag.

"You're a gorgeous Falastiniyya. *Mashallah*. Let's go."

Chapter 50

Alya: Maftool

Alya busied herself making *maftool*. She'd take her time. She began by sifting the wheat flour. It passed smoothly through the sieve. Next, she added a few drops of water and hand-rolled the wheat and bulgur into tiny pasta pearls.

As she worked, Alya thought about the March. She had wanted to join the human chain, but instead found herself at home, wondering if the protesters were safe. Abdullah persuaded her not to go by promising another trip to Al-Quds. They'd be hungry when they got home, and this was the perfect dish for the occasion.

She'd made *maftool* practically her whole life. She could make it in her sleep.

Once she finished making the pasta pearls, she steamed them over boiling water and began preparing the topping. Amer loved it when she placed the pumpkin right in the center of the *maftool* tray. He'd always bring her a small pumpkin for the dish, smiling as he said, "This reminds me of the pumpkins we grew back home. It tastes like honey." He'd smack his lips in delight, unable to hide his pleasure.

He never stopped calling Al-Majdal home.

She drained the chickpeas and began washing the pumpkin, onions, tomatoes, and zucchini. The kids didn't like most of those vegetables. She tried to entice them by saying their grandpa loved to eat them all, but it didn't always work.

Cutting up the vegetables, she entertained herself by singing.

"Ya Falastina, Ya Falastina, you're the shining sun.

Ya Falastina, your love is deep in my heart.

Ya Falastine, I'll etch your name on the sun that doesn't set.

You're more precious than my money and my children."

After lightly roasting the chicken, Alya turned off the oven and sat down to wait for everyone to arrive. It was 4 p.m., just minutes before the call to Asr prayer. She laid the prayer rug in front of her. It was thick black velvet with an image of the Kaaba at its centre, a gift from Adla after her pilgrimage to Mecca.

Alya remembered prostrating during prayers at Al-Aqsa. She didn't know how she managed to bend her knees that way. Now, her legs ached again. Nevertheless, she stood barefoot on the prayer rug, her feet soothed by the velvet, then lowered herself into a sitting position.

The *adhan* would be any minute now. The *muezzin* who called the prayer at the nearby mosque had a melodious, vibrant voice. Throughout the day or evening, whether Alya was caught up in a chore or lost in thought, the call to prayer would break her from her toil. Its cadence always provided her with a quiet steadiness.

Alya only realized she had dozed off when she opened her eyes to the call of "Allahu Akbar!" She tried to determine whether it was the *adhan* or the protesters' chants. Voices continued to ring in her ears, shouting "Allahu Akbar!"

Pushing herself up, she walked to the window as the voices echoed outside. As Alya slid the window open, the whistling of wings fluttered past her ears. A white dove flew away and soared above. The chants grew louder, yet no one was in sight. Glancing around, Alya searched for the source of the shouts.

Making her way downstairs, she stepped outside. The branches of the lemon tree in the front yard swayed. A light breeze stirred, and the dried leaves beneath the tree danced.

She looked up to see Amer smiling down at her. He was plowing with his hoe and singing:

"Ya Falastina, Ya Falastina, you're the shining sun.

Ya Falastina, your love is deep in my heart."

Acknowledgements

It has been a rough journey, paved with uncertainty and relentless hurdles. I came to learn that the most precarious conditions of life were the pains of labor that would give birth to this book. A fierce force formed within, propelling me to hold on and keep writing. Writing amid attacks, fear, and unpredictability, I had to shield the light in my heart from being extinguished and the oxygen in my soul from fading. I was treading the path of darkness and loneliness, finding solace only in the nobility of my mission.

Writing has been a lonely path, with no audience to applaud or followers to parade my work before. Yet I'm deeply grateful to have come across a few people who helped me along the way.

First, I'd like to express my sincere thanks to my family, who supported me every step of the way, especially my siblings Mohanad and Reham. Their constructive feedback and unwavering encouragement motivated me in immeasurable ways. My thanks also go to my friends who generously gave me their time and support: Tarneem Hammad, Kevin Hadduck, Don Jacques, and Adria Arafat.

I'm grateful to my colleagues in the Creative Writing Master's Program at the University of Hull for two years of honest, constructive feedback. I'm especially thankful to my professors at Hull for their professional and moral support.

My gratitude also goes to Ramsey Hanhan, a fellow Palestinian author I got to know by reading his book.

Finally, I'd like to thank my meticulous and professional editor, Izabela Shubair, whose invaluable insight helped shape *And No Net Ensnares Me* into a stronger version of itself. I'm also grateful to Fomite Press for believing this book could make a difference in the world, and to Donna Bister for bringing its visual life to fruition with such care.

About the Author

Rana Shubair is a Palestinian writer. She specializes in English language training, testing and translation. Working with young people has given her the chance to understand their dreams and the energy that lies within. She sees her job as a chance to instill hope and motivation in their lives so they may take towards accomplishing their dreams.

Rana has lived through all the turbulences and major events, which took place in her country. The intelligent youth of Gaza persevering under the Siege and the stalwart widows who struggle to care for their children have all inspired her to tell the world her story. Rana currently lives in Gaza with her family and has lived a part of her life in the USA.

Rana started writing at a young age and published works on women and Gaza on numerous websites like opendemocracy.net. She's a mother of three and hopes one day her children will travel to see the world that exists outside Gaza.

She is the author of I*n Gaza I Dare to Dream*, and *My Lover is a Freedom Fighter.*

More novels and novellas from Fomite...

Joshua Amses — *During This, Our Nadir*
Joshua Amses — *Ghats*
Joshua Amses — *Raven or Crow*
Joshua Amses — *The Moment Before an Injury*
Charles Bell — *The Married Land*
Charles Bell — *The Half Gods*
Jaysinh Birjepatel — *Nothing Beside Remains*
Jaysinh Birjepatel — *The Good Muslim of Jackson Heights*
David Borofka — *The End of Good Intnetions*
David Brizer — *The Secret Doctrine of V. H. Rand*
David Brizer — *Victor Rand*
L. M Brown — *Hinterland*
Paula Closson Buck — *Summer on the Cold War Planet*
L.enny Cavallaro — *Paganini Agitato*
Dan Chodorkoff — *Loisaida*
Dan Chodorkoff — *Sugaring Down*
David Adams Cleveland — *Time's Betrayal*
Paul Cody— *Sphyxia*
Jaimee Wriston Colbert — *Vanishing Acts*
Roger Coleman — *Skywreck Afternoons*
Stephen Downes — *The Hands of Pianists*
Marc Estrin — *Hyde*
Marc Estrin — *Kafka's Roach*
Marc Estrin — *Proceedings of the Hebrew Free Burial Society*
Marc Estrin — *Speckled Vanities*
Marc Estrin — *The Annotated Nose*
Marc Estrin — *The Penseés of Alan Krieger*
Zdravka Evtimova — *Asylum for Men and Dogs*
Zdravka Evtimova — *In the Town of Joy and Peace*
Zdravka Evtimova — *Sinfonia Bulgarica*
Zdravka Evtimova — *You Can Smile on Wednesdays*
Daniel Forbes — *Derail This Train Wreck*
Peter Fortunato — *Carnevale*
Greg Guma — *Dons of Time*
Ramsey Hanhan – *Fugitive Dreams*

Fomite

Fomite